THE FORESTS OF ELYSIA

Bizar[illegible] Ti[illegible]

by

Terry Dunn

illustrations by

Phoebe Moon

To

Dear Sharon

Thank you so much for your help. You're a star!

With lots of love

from Gilly xx

TWO STAR PUBLICATIONS

Bizarh Times
ISBN 0 954 2633 0 8

Published by Two Star Publications
100 La Collette Flats
Green Street
St. Helier
JERSEY
JE2 4UP

Design & production co-ordinated by:
The ***Better Book*** Company Ltd
Warblington Lodge
Havant
Hampshire PO9 2XH

Illustrations by Phoebe Moon

Printed in England

Contents

The artwork in this book is dedicated to my late grandmother, Irene Iris Le Mesurier.
"Where would I have been without you gran"

PHOEBE MOON 2003

Acknowledgements

I would like to thank my son Brett and my family for their continuous support.

Also grateful thanks to John and Jan Nicolas, Ruby Hayes, Joy Couillard, Eric Nicolas, Sheila Veal and Sue Monet.

Finally, love and thanks to my partner, Arthur Le Cornu, who after many years of acclimatization can now walk confidently into a household of dragons, unicorns, talking cats and singing hamsters.

I am very grateful to them all.

Gill Hudson
May 2003

Author:

TERRY DUNN

Illustrator:

PHOEBE MOON

"Bart" courtesy of Jersey Falconry

Photograph by Eric Nicolas

THE KINGDOM OF ELYSIA
TRADERSHIPS ON COASTAL WATERS
BOG & MARSHLAND
GREAT LAKE
THE GREAT FORESTS OF ELYSIA
TALLA-WEYRE
ELFIN VILLAGES
WHISPERING SPIRES
UNICORN GLADE
PHOEBE MOON 2000 ©

Introduction

This is a story of quest, peril, heroism and self-discovery in a land where magic is the domain of the few. Where most creatures are sentient beings, Unicorns still thrive in vast, uncharted forests, and dragons are the pinnacle of animal evolution.

This then is the forest kingdom of Elysia, where an all threatening blight has been unwittingly released upon the land. A blight that spells doom for one and all.

And this is where a band of great dragons along with their Royal Majesties and several timid forest dwellers set out to put right this wrong. Along the way they encounter various strange beings.

A mysterious, telepathic Elfin beauty with an unknown, unspoken connection with the King, wildwood faeries of fearful reputation, isolated and sinister looking castles, mercenary Elves and a dark wizard with evil plans of his own.

Before this book evolved Phoebe Moon's artwork had only been available at craft fairs and through private commissions, however in 1997 it was decided a story should be written around some of her characters and a search for the ideal author began.

Hence Terry Dunn, who has written short stories and articles for specialist magazines was chosen and between them Terry and Phoebe set about creating the mystical world of Elysia...

1

Three Spells Too Many

It was night time in the forests of Elysia.

The twin moons were full and both smiled down onto the green canopy and the creatures in and beneath it that were active between dusk and dawn. From the lower forms, the unnoticed and unnamed crawlers that pushed, burrowed and hunted among the leaf mulch, bracken and damp hollows, to the more intelligent, sometimes sentient ones that ran and leapt between the trunks and boughs.

Into this latter bracket fell the moongliders, frolicking among the high branches and flitting from tree top to tree top. Charming and amiable creatures, they slept in daylight with their brilliant, incandescent wings outstretched to absorb the golden rays of the sun, storing up its energy like solar cells to give them the power of flight during the hours of darkness. Soft furred, light boned and with a firm grip and prehensile tail, they were a perfect adaptation to night life in the trees. Likewise their eyes which, in order to see in the dark with clarity enough to leap confidently from tree to tree, had adjusted to see not just the normal spectrum of light but on into the higher, ethereal bands.

Not many knew this fact although the creatures themselves were commonplace among the forests of Elysia. Indeed, a large colony of moongliders sunning their wings while asleep in the noonday sun could make a section of forest or a single tree sparkle in multicoloured hues like a huge kaleidoscope. A dazzling sight that took the breath away. It was another common trait of these creatures to see them, during their night activities, occasionally freeze and raise their faces to the heavens. The generally accepted explanation among those who witnessed this action was that the tree dwellers were simply sniffing the air to try and locate other moongliders or detect any other approaching creatures.

But they weren't sniffing at all. They were looking up.

At the magic in the air.

In one part of the deep forest a small number of moongliders stopped briefly and looked down. Even though to the normal eye the view below was swathed in impenetrable blackness where the moonlight did not reach the forest floor, the moongliders could clearly see the dragon there. And no ordinary dragon either.

Instantly recognizable to the watchers the sleeping dragon, coiled up in a great circular nest of bracken at the base of three huge oaks, was unaware of his observation. He was a handsome beast, his emerald green scales and smooth, supple wing membranes shouted his health and fitness. He was a big dragon too. What was known in Elysia as a dragon of stature, and these were few.

Just to see a dragon in the forest was itself strange, which may explain how he came to have the name Bizarh. Strange because as far as was known, Bizarh was the only living forest dragon. All other dragons, especially dragons of stature, were to be found in the villages and towns and in the company of folk. Yet somehow he alone had arrived deep in the greenwood.

The moongliders, cloud-hoppers, unicorns and other sentient forest dwellers had their own ideas on this puzzle. They believed he was an accident.

Every fifty years the mature dragons of Elysia pair up and mate before the females fly off to the distant mountains to lay their hard, granite-like eggs among the high crags. The forest creatures believe that one female, cutting it a bit too fine on her nesting flight, had produced her first egg too soon and it had dropped into the forest, immediately lost to her amongst the dense foliage and undergrowth. And so the wayward egg had lain like a stone for its ten year incubation period, growing mosses and lichens, being roosted on by birds and crawled over by insects, until the young Bizarh hatched out.

He had grown fit and strong in the forests, protected during his vulnerable infancy by its impenetrability, and through the years had come to know the way of the wildwoods. He was a friend to the beasts of the land no matter how big or small and his skin had gradually taken on the hue of his environment to give him his unusual and extremely striking colouring.

The younger members of the watching moongliders were tempted to wake the sleeping dragon. They liked to tease him when a chance arose. Sometimes they would drop nuts or fruit onto him while he was trying to contemplate some deep thought. This intrusion would break his concentration and he would slyly glance up into the night. If he could see the little silhouettes against the sky and was sure they were safely out of reach he would puff out a spurt of flame. Just a brief flash, more light than heat and barely enough to singe the lower leaves. The moongliders would screech in mock terror and fly to the highest branches. Bizarh would roar with laughter and move off in search of a quieter spot for his contemplations.

And so the little moongliders did not disturb Bizarh's slumbers. They loved him for his caring ways and gentle nature. It was a mark of their respect for him that they curbed their normally mischievous ways and left the sleeping leviathan to his dreams.

Much nearer to the edge of the dense forest, in the wooded hinterland that separated the more heavy and in places almost impenetrable forest proper from the surrounding plains tilled by the lowland Elfin folk, was an open place of quiet solace.

Accessible enough to the more determined of those who walked on two legs, whenever they were in need of wise advice or even help from a well meted magic spell, the white buildings that filled the middle of the space inspired awe and respect. With its towers and broad gardens it was a place where the breeze could finally penetrate the high forest canopy and gather some speed across the ground. This rare, refreshing ground breeze sighed between the tall structures before being soaked up by the surrounding foliage, the softly changing tones it made giving rise to the name of the place. Whispering Spires. A place of tranquillity, peaceful enough even to tempt in those most shy of all forest creatures, the Unicorns. They had been known to visit on occasion, when the bi-peds were not around on a visit to the one who lived there. Visiting because the Whispering Spires were home to the usually helpful, often generous and much respected Elfin wizard Oaken-Pel.

At first glance Oaken-Pel appeared to be a slim, unassuming man. He still had the hawk nose and the all round facial hair of normal Elfin folk, but seemed to carry himself with a quiet proudness, this emphasized by his height. It was a strange thing but Elfin wizards always seemed to be taller than the average. It wasn't that those who were naturally taller were chosen or set out to become wizards. More that wizards just seem to develop a sort of 'tallness'. Perhaps this was a by-product of being a dealer in the magic arts? Who could say, but dealing in magic was what Oaken-Pel was in the process of doing at that very moment.

A delegation of elders from one of the more local villages, still a good day and a half of hard travel distant from the Whispering Spires, had earlier approached him. The village crops had suffered from a dry spell after the collapse of the local dam which diverted water to their irrigation system. The dam had of course been repaired, but it had taken several crucial weeks and by the time water was restored the damage had been done. Loss of their crops would mean terrible winter hardships and so, as a last resort, they had come to Oaken-Pel. In return for whatever he asked, could he cast a spell to speed up the last few weeks of crop growth in their fields so their produce would be ready to sell at the time of the big markets?

Oaken-Pel had just smiled. How could he object, this was clearly a justified use of magic. Yes, he could do it, and in return all he asked was that a small group of the village Elves visit the Whispering Spires now and then to tend his gardens and keep them neat, tidy and weed free. The wizard did not explain why he wished this simple task done, but he alone knew that the Unicorns did so enjoy grazing on the sweet, lush green lawns beneath the spires without having to pick their way between the weeds and other wild plants that were not to their tastes. It was this that tempted them out from the deep woods and away from their own secret glades and the wizard never ceased to be charmed and enthralled to catch sight of one of these beautiful, elusive creatures.

The deal was duly struck and on Oaken-Pel's instructions the elders returned to their village with the promise that he would generate and send the growing spell this very night.

Now, wizards, like dragons, are not exactly thick on the ground in Elysia and it is also not as common as is generally thought that strong magic is actually used.

The peoples of Elysia, from the highest positions of the royal court right down to the unassuming wild faeries that inhabit the dark woods, go about their normal daily business without relying on magic at all. Tilling the land, bartering with other villages, going to the trade fairs and visiting the regular grand market in the great city were things that went on with scant regard for the higher abilities. Magic was still an honoured and respected skill, wizards always commanded respect whenever they were seen in public, but it fell far short of the real reverence, honour, allegiance and love given to the King and Queen of Elysia by their people. Wizards and their use of magic had their place in Elysia, but they were by no means commonplace.

Yet this coming night was to witness even more magic, for a second spell was already in the process of being prepared.

On the far side of the great forest, to the east where it was already beginning to get dark on the western faces of the mountains, another wizard was at work.

Tourmalane liked it in the mountains. He was left alone, a virtual recluse, only going down into the valley for occasional provisions and to collect the odd, special items needed for his growing collections of speciality spells. For that was his passion and his chosen field of study. And tonight was the time for one of those spells.

In the steeply sloping gardens of his rather modest house, well, modest for a wizard, he was in the process of adding another building, specially designed to hold, store and give him space enough to experiment with all his magic components.

Erecting a building with the use of magic was not beyond the talents of a skilled and experienced wizard. And he had done it because he was no builder and certainly would not have allowed strangers to invade his privacy, let alone run willy-nilly around his property. But the hard part was keeping it there. So Tourmalane was in the process of creating a special, non reversible spell. Once his new building was charged with this it would then be as safe as, well, houses.

Tonight, when the moons were high, he would project his spell and watch in delight as his magic worked its way into the stonework. The play of ethereal light that sparked and fizzed when magic did its stuff was one of Tourmalane's great pleasures, a pleasure he could enjoy all to himself in the solitude of his mountain eyrie.

Yes, across the length and breadth of Elysia things were going on as they had done since before living memory. Life seemed idyllic and orderly enough for those that lived there. The sentient beings knew their place and the steady stream of existence slid along with barely a ripple in the flow.

Yet not everyone was happy with their lot. Of course, this was natural enough and many of those in Elysia hoped and planned to improve both themselves and their situations. These individual hopes and aspirations were known to some but ignored by most. One creature's business was his and his alone.

But a wise old wizard had once said :-

'All it takes for evil to flourish is for good men to do nothing.' And in one particular, dark place, evil was indeed flourishing.

Hard against the dark edge of the great forest, between the last of the trees and the wide expanse of mist shrouded bog lands was a great lake. It seemed to just hunker there between the greyness and the green wood, keeping the two apart as if trying to prevent them from fighting.

This boggy swampland, shrouded in both mists and superstition, was a place rarely visited and the Elfin tribe that lived along its edge was easily recognized. They had a certain smell, a certain look and a particularly surly disposition. And they always kept one watchful eye on the lake. Or to be more precise, the island at its centre.

Wide as the waters were, this dark, brooding place could be seen from anywhere along the shoreline. Even when the swampland mists grew thick enough to spill out across the water the dark towers of the fortress at the top of the island pierced their way up through the fog. The sun never seemed to shine directly onto the fortress and the rumours say it is because the blackness of the stonework reflected the black heart of the wizard who lived there.

Although he seemed just a story to frighten small children to those who lived far away, to those who lived around the lakeside and under his shadow Goth was real enough and a wizard to be feared.

These fears were well placed for, bad though he was, wizard Goth chose this particular night for one of his most dastardly deeds. Having been crossed once too often by the head Elf of the villagers that fished the lake around his island, this 'puny' fisher Elf was about to feel the wizard's wrath.

Goth had been cheated. And more than once in his opinion, but this last outrage was the last straw.

The lakeside elves fished the murky waters for the plentiful cruiser fish that sucked in huge quantities of water as they swam, filtering out not just the krill, shrimp and other small life forms that were their food, but also the small amounts of minerals permanently in liquid suspension there too. The elves had had a recent run of good fortune and managed to catch several very old cruisers. Despite being perhaps hundreds of years old their flesh was still edible and ended up on the market stalls as usual. But inside the swim bladders of these fish was the accumulation of minerals, built up over the many years, the bulk of which was the heaviest, inert metal used by the fish as naturally acquired ballast.

Gold!

Now normally the fisher Elves collected up all the small amounts of this precious metal from perhaps half a year's catches and used it to buy supplementary items to improve their village life. But this latest catch of several very old cruisers together had rendered up a veritable fortune, even with the percentage given in tribute to the

King, which no one begrudged anyway.

But Goth felt he had been cheated out of *his* share. And this wasn't the first time he'd been cheated either. After all, it was his lake. He'd never seen a single groat from all the past catches of gold granules, let alone a percentage of the sales of his fish. Now he had been deprived of part of a fortune in gold.

Tonight the Elfin folk of the lake would celebrate their windfall. Goth, of course, had not been invited and was in no mood for good cheer. His wrath was centred on the village leader. He controlled his village and so he was to blame. And tonight he must pay.

Thus, in the twilight of his fortress, Goth was preparing the most potent, almost never used and most reviled of all magic spells. The spell that went against the whole creed of wizardhood. The spell normally not allowed to be used without express permission from the King.

The spell that kills.

And so this fateful night fell. A night that would have dire consequences for Elysia.

In the great forests the night creatures were stirring as those of the sun settled to their slumbers. The moongliders began to awake from their daytime rest and recharge as the nimble cloud-hoppers, their daylight counterparts who took it upon themselves to watch over any of the night rovers who might be resting nearby during their daytime reposes, bedded down among the soft mosses. Translucent wings were flexed and movement could soon be heard in the high branches as the first moongliders to awake began to move off on their nocturnal forages.

All this was going on unsuspecting and in total innocence while three totally different wizards in equally different far flung corners of Elysia began their preparations for the execution of their spells. And prepare they must for serious spells were hard work.

People think magicians can just trot out spells willy-nilly, or abracadabra if you like. Not so. Only small, insignificant spells, usually those pre-prepared purely for show or demonstration purposes, could be cast straight from the hand. Proper spells of any true weight had to be drawn up from within the wizard. The sorcerer had to 'power up' his own aura and use part of it to launch the spell. The individual spells could thus be attributed to the actual wizards who cast them because the residue of the magic held a segment of its sender's aura. All this information is useless of course, unless you can see these auras and as far as was known to the peoples of Elysia, the only sentient beings with the ability to see into the ethereal bands of light were the wizards themselves.

Unintentionally, but in unison, Oaken-Pel, Tourmalane and Goth all stood in full regalia before an open window. Each uttered their cadences, gestured with wide arm movements over their selected magical components and drew from deep within themselves the mystic power that fate and the Gods had bestowed upon them. That uncanny power which enabled the lucky few to use magic. The same power that fuelled their much greater than normal auras.

For them everything was coming together to enable each to produce and project spells of weight. The conjunction of the three vital ingredients that all skilled exponents of magic understood were essential. A true 'weighty' spell needed firstly solid, good quality components or ingredients. Secondly, great aura power and thirdly, velocity. Big spells needed to gather speed, hence the open windows.

The unfortunate and unintentional fourth ingredient about to be added to this already potent mix was unison, because no more than one spell can occupy any single given moment in time and space. They react unpredictably if several are attempted to be forced together. Strange things can happen.

Unknowing, as one the three wizards called aloud their final chants, drew up their powers and at the same moment thrust their arms out at the night sky, launching the magic into the darkness.

A few seconds later each of the three bearded faces registered baffled surprise. As per normal the spells rifled out into the night, coloured auras streaming out behind them like comet tails. Then, expecting them to gather speed out over the forest before turning in the direction they were meant to go then swooping down to their targets and do their jobs, the wizards were quite shocked when the magic didn't.

Drawn to each other by some unknown magic-netic force, somehow produced by three powerful spells in the ether all at once, the magic comets fired straight off into the distance and in a few moments were gone from sight.

Oaken-Pel, Tourmalane and even black hearted Goth were frozen in a stunned silence, gazing out of their windows at the suddenly empty sky.

Far, far out over the vastness of the forests of Elysia the spells flew out over great tracts of greenwood so dense that no bi-ped had as yet explored it. Each was now on a collision course with the others.

Down below, in the untamed wildwoods the night creatures moved about their business in blissful ignorance of what went on overhead. Of the imminent collision. In fact most would just carry on unaware even after it, at least for a short while.

Then, it happened.

The three different spells came together with a stunning impact of magic and to those around who *could* see into the ethereal band, the sky exploded into light with a blinding flash of deafening silence. The moongliders screeched in fear, their screams rolling out through the forest as the light hit them, the frightened, dazzled creatures shielding their eyes from the suddenly blinding heavens. The other forest creatures, unable to see what had caused their distress, but instinctively recognizing the sound of real fear, froze in a state of alert and for a long moment the entire forests of Elysia were completely motionless.

Now locked together into one space as a tri-spell the out of control knot of magic, robbed of all its speed, crashed down through the canopy to the forest floor fizzing and spitting multi-hued sparks of ethereal light before finally settling into a duller, pulsating sizzle. A seething ball of uncontrolled energy, it began to eat its way into the ground, sinking as a lump of ice might disappear when placed on a hot plate. After a few moments it was gone from sight, apparently absorbed into the very soil.

The three wizards back out on the edges of the forest saw the white impact flash, far away on the horizon. Perhaps half a minute later a faint animal cry reached their ears. Right behind it came a silence so complete that it jangled the nerves. Then once again, as one they turned from the open windows and retired to their prospective studies, each intent on going over his spell preparations to try and determine just what had gone wrong.

Still, no harm done.

* * * * *

"Wake up."

It was a quiet, quite high pitched and timid voice, unlikely to wake anyone. It didn't.

"Wake up." There was a little more volume then and the timid tone was still there, but urgency was also making itself known.

The call still got no visible response from the hulking form of a slumbering Bizarh who, although the sun was already rising over the tops of the eastern mountains, had chosen this bright morning to sleep late.

The small, russet coloured deer-like creature looked on at the huge coiled mass for several impatient minutes before trying again. No matter how big or fearsome the dragon, she thought, there was no need for rudeness. It's not nice to be ignored, especially when you've come a long way with something important to say. She stamped her little hooves, waggled her antennae then vibrated her small gossamer wings until they sang like the hum of bees. All of this did absolutely nothing to wake the sleeper.

But small creatures of the forest are quite capable of making loud noises, usually as a defence mechanism or as a signal of alert.

The little deer took a deep breath.

"WAKE UP!"

The shout filled the immediate area and surrounding forest, flushing several scarlet coloured Swirler birds up into the sky and sending nearby ground crawlers scurrying for cover.

Bizarh jolted out of his slumber, opened one eye and slowly uncoiled with barely a rustle from his scales.

"Hu... huh?"

His other eye cracked open, squinting against the more direct sunlight on that side. Then he slowly sat back on his haunches, pushed his forelegs forward, stretched his long neck towards the sky, spread his leathery wings to their full extension and opened his jaws wide in a fang filled yawn that was the culmination of a truly gargantuan stretch.

"Yesss..." His voice was a mixture of enjoyment and satisfaction. "Now, what was that noise?"

Looking around he could see no one. At first the surrounding woods seemed undisturbed but for the flapping birds. Then, to his front, right at the edge of the forest, a large clump of ferns quivered slightly.

"Hullo, what have we here then?" His voice was soft. "It's all right little fellow. You can come on out, I won't hurt you."

The last part of the sentence was really unnecessary. At least to all the creatures who knew of this forest dragon and were well aware of his pacifist nature. But he still struck an impressive, imposing and often intimidating figure to those smaller than himself, which was just about everyone else in the forest.

He waited patiently and after a few moments the little winged deer emerged from between the parting fronds. She shivered in trepidation and did not fully leave the fern clump, as if it offered some form of protection from the giant before her. Bizarh dropped effortlessly back down onto all fours and lowered his head to eye the creature nearer its own level.

"A cloud-hopper! Well, this is a surprise. So, what can I do for you?" Bizarh offered a friendly grin which did nothing to bolster the cloud-hopper's already almost non-existent confidence, several rows of gleaming, pointed teeth did not cheer. The little deer suddenly saw itself as a possible snack and it took every ounce of nerve not to immediately flit away into the cover of the trees.

"I... I'm sorry. Sorry I woke you."

"That's all right." Bizarh briefly scanned the forest, looking for any nearby metallic shine. "Where are the moongliders? I thought you looked after them while they slept?"

This got a nod of confirmation.

" Yes, but they are the ones who sent me here. Binnie, they said, go and get Bizarh. He'll know what to do."

"I will? With what?" Bizarh's scaly eyebrows went up. Just a few moments old and it was already proving to be an interesting morning.

"With what is happening in the forest. In the deep forest. You have to come and see."

"I do, do I?"

"Yes, yes!" There was no denying the urgency in the high pitched voice.

Bizarh sighed and cocked his head to one side, considering. He had no plans for the day but whatever cloud-hoppers or moongliders thought was vitally important usually turned out to be extremely trivial. Still, the little deer seemed earnest enough.

"All right then, Binnie," he said, rather magnanimously. "If you say so. Where to?"

This took the edge off Binnie's fear and she flicked her head to one side.

"Follow me."

She flexed her legs and sprung into the air, gossamer wings blurring into action with their characteristic hum. Without a backward glance, glad just to be out from under the dragon's glare, she rose up into the air, resting momentarily in the top of the nearest tree to make sure he was following, then set off towards the deep woods, skimming just above the tops of the trees.

In complete contrast to the cloud-hopper's somewhat delicate, elegant, yet effort filled take off, Bizarh coiled, launched and swooped straight up into the blue, just a few beats of his broad wings gaining him several hundred feet of altitude. He circled lazily in the steadily warming air and watched the cloud-hopper skipping over the trees, leapfrogging along in a series of short duration flights. To a natural flyer like Bizarh the halting progress of the little deer seemed painfully slow, but he knew it was just their way. Only able to manage short distances, their flight capability was really only one of escape or evasion, not a proper form of travel.

After perhaps an hour or so of this halting travel the cloud-hopper settled onto a thick branch nearer the ground for a rest. Bizarh swooped down and landed beside the tree, crushing several small saplings in the process and nearly blasting the little deer from her perch with the down draught from his wings. He wasn't even breathing hard while the cloud-hopper panted frantically and looked exhausted.

"How much further is it?" he asked after giving the little deer a few minutes to recover.

"Well, it took me over two days to reach you." Binnie was rather proud of her efforts. "Where we have to go is way out in the wild woods. I hope it's not too far for you?"

Another time Bizarh might have laughed, but he realized at that moment that for any cloud-hopper to make such an effort of what was for her long distance travel, let alone leave their beloved moongliders, there must be something out of the ordinary going on. It was his first inkling that this 'whatever it was' looked like being more than just the silly games and tricks the moongliders liked to play on him. Time perhaps to speed things up and get to where he was being led to just a tad quicker.

"Right then." For the first time Binnie noted a tone of seriousness in the dragon's voice. "Let's get a move on." He dipped one shoulder. "Up you go."

"Wh... what?"

"Jump on." Bizarh shrugged the shoulder. "We'll make much better time if I carry you, so up you go." The cloud hopper clearly wasn't too keen on the idea. "Come on, I won't eat you." If it was meant as a joke it fell flat, another toothy grin not helping either and the little deer looking very nervous indeed. Bizarh dropped his shoulder even lower. "I promise," he added in his best sincere voice and sidled in until his shoulder bumped against Binnie's branch. She really had no choice then and slowly, tentatively stepped onto the green, scaly back. It wasn't anything like she'd imagined. Not rough and hard at all, but slightly supple and surprisingly warm to the touch.

"Best if you lay down." Bizarh curved his long neck around and the little deer suddenly found herself gazing straight into one huge eye. She watched the lens with its strange crystalline structure flex as it adjusted to focus on her. But there was no hint of menace there, just genuine good intentions. For the first time she began not to feel in imminent danger and started to relax. Just a little.

"I'll try to keep it as level as I can. Just shout which way you want me to go, all right?"

The little deer could only nod dumbly in reply, still shocked at her own bravery. She doubted any cloud-hopper had ever been this close to a dragon, let alone fly upon its back or even steer it and even before the dragon took flight there was a rush of exhilaration from deep within her. This was instantly quashed the moment Bizarh coiled and launched, the sudden jerk of it almost dislodging her and she hung on for dear life as the winged behemoth beneath her climbed into the sky.

In moments the cloud-hopper was higher than any cloud-hopper had ever been and as Bizarh levelled off at almost a thousand feet and spread his wings wide, settling into a smooth glide, Binnie peered carefully over the curve of his shoulder and stared down open mouthed at the vast expanse of glorious greenness that was Elysia. She'd never realized it was *so* big!

Bizarh felt the little hooves grip even tighter, digging into the joints between his scales.

"Are you all right?" he asked, his voice coming easily over the soft whoosh of the slipstream, but apparently going unheeded. Once again he swivelled his neck and eyed the little deer. "What's wrong?"

Little Binnie, the unassuming and timid cloud-hopper, looked now at Bizarh with new eyes. What a great privilege to experience this, and what a truly great thing it must be to be a dragon of stature.

"Yes. Yes... I'm all right. It's just... so high."

Bizarh laughed.

"Well I promise not to crash into any hard clouds. Now, which way?"

After a brief pause, while Binnie scanned the ground below to get her bearings, she pointed off with her snout, away towards the darker forest on the horizon. Bizarh just grinned that fanged grin before stretching out his head and neck into a single graceful line. Then he carefully banked to the right, adopted a slightly inclined attitude and began to increase speed, playing with consummate ease his shallow dive against the rising warm air from the greenery below. The little deer crouched low on the scaly back between the broad shoulders and to her surprise found her own nose also automatically turning to point into the rushing slipstream.

The unlikely pair flew on for much of the rest of the day with only infrequent returns to the ground. Despite his considerable weight Bizarh could keep himself aloft for long periods. He had an almost uncanny knack of being able to locate thermals and soar inside them. Thus their cross forest travel consisted of a series of high, spiralling soars, each followed by a long, descending glide. The high altitudes Bizarh could reach took Little Binnie's breath away and the great swoops back down across vast tracts of forest that would normally take her as long as an hour to cross exhilarated her as the distance was now covered in just a few minutes.

By mid-afternoon they were over very dense forests. Forests that even Bizarh had never been to before. It was so thick in places as to almost become jungle. As the green dragon casually scanned the lands ahead his attention was caught by a strange discolouration up ahead. His eyes became fully focused upon it as they flew on. As the change became more defined it shocked him. Shocked them both.

Binnie hadn't realized just how extensive the damage was. Bizarh simply had trouble understanding just what he was seeing. Adjusting his angle of attack into the slipstream he began to beat his wings and climbed higher for a better view.

Beneath them, in a great circle over a dozen miles across, the rich green of the forest had turned a dull, lifeless brown. Not just the trees in it were dead, but every living thing. The dragon jackknifed into a steep dive and with Binnie hanging on went into a steep dive, using his higher speed to circle the edge of the brownness after levelling off at a couple of hundred feet. It still took several long minutes to fly right around the perimeter, all the while the pair looking on in silence.

The brown area was indeed dead. The trees within it were completely lifeless, many already fully decayed and fallen, something that would naturally take dozens of years.

"How long... ?" Bizarh's voice was subdued.

"According to the moongliders, it's only about four days old," came the equally quiet reply. "That's why I was sent."

The dragon swooped in even lower for one more pass before banking away and heading earthward. He skilfully stalled just above the ground and landed right at the edge of the brownness, taking care though to touch down just inside the greenwood. Binnie lifted away from her scaly perch and floated to the ground beside him, standing in silence as he leant forward, out over the brownness, and gingerly touched the dead plants. It did not feel dangerous. He stepped out of the green and onto the brown soil, ready at the instant to lift off if necessary. Nothing happened and after a minute he bent his long neck down to more closely inspect the soil. Not a single plant lived. No grasses, ferns, mosses, weeds or even lichen survived. Nothing. After seeing that it did not appear to adversely affect the big dragon, Binnie walked out on to the brownness too and stood beside Bizarh's head, easily as big as her entire body. Her fear of him was forgotten as one huge eye turned its focus on her.

"Things just don't die this quickly, Binnie." The big dragon said.

"Yes. The moongliders say it is inside the earth itself."

"What is?"

"The bad magic."

It had to be, Bizarh realized. Nothing else could be this powerful or work so quickly. But who would do such a thing? He nodded to himself then straightened.

"Let's find the moongliders and see what they have to say ..."

Any more words remained unsaid as he turned to step back into the greenwood they had left just moments before. It was now ten feet away from them and all the trees and plants in between were already withered.

"By the twin moons!" he gasped.

"Let's go," begged the suddenly frightened Binnie. "I don't like it. Please, we could both be dead any moment."

"If it's in the soil we're safe enough," said Bizarh. "But if this isn't stopped, and soon, none of Elysia's forest will be safe. And if the forests die..." He stopped in mid sentence again as the sudden enormity of the impending disaster struck home. It was too horrible to contemplate.

"Stop it? But how?"

Bizarh shook his head, realizing with more horror that he did not know how.

"Come on, let's find the moongliders and see what they know. Then we'll decide what to do next."

Both creatures lifted off from the scorched earth and without any bidding made sure their feet were dirt free before turning out over the endangered green forest in search of a metallic shine.

It didn't take them too long, after all, Binnie was a cloud-hopper. Everyone knew they naturally paired up with moongliders and that it was their main task and joy to watch over their sleeping partners while they re-charged during the daylight hours. Only two things were normally powerful enough to make the little deer leave their charges. The first was danger of immediate death, and the second, of all things, was the sight of a rainbow. It appeared the arching rays of multi-coloured light had some hypnotic effect on the creatures. Some unstoppable urge possessed them and drew them towards the beautiful bands of colour. They just couldn't help themselves. This of course left the sleeping moongliders totally unguarded, although in reality they were in little danger. They had no natural predators and poaching was now virtually a thing of the past. But it had not always been so. Once upon a time it had been a real enough danger.

The metallic wings of moongliders were, and still are, much prized. More valuable even than gold, the metallic shine is a symbol of real wealth among the Elfin folk of Elysia.

Nowadays, and by order of the King no less, only the wings of moongliders who died naturally could be turned into cloth or goods. And as moongliders lived mostly in the deep forests very few wings ever turned up, making them a rare and precious commodity. But when they did they were turned by specialist master craftsmen into small items of clothing and more usually brooches or other jewellery. Because of the material's rarity, great value and beauty, someone who sported a piece of moonglider wing jewellery was clearly a person of wealth. By this same token Elfin folk had been known to travel many days to a place where it was known the King was to make a personal appearance just to get a glimpse of his magnificent, virtually priceless and visually stunning moonglider wing cape. The only one of its kind in existence and a sight to dazzle the eye as he passed by, the silvery fineness of the metallic cloth glinted in a multitude of colours as it rippled in the breeze.

But before the order of the King had become law, black market moonglider wings had been making unscrupulous poachers rich and put the inoffensive little night flyers in deadly peril. That was also the time when the cloud-hoppers had first allied themselves to the moongliders as their protectors, raising the alarm when danger was near.

Once this terrible practice had been brought to the attention of the King and Queen, who were both horrified, the royal house immediately brought in the new law, putting a stop to it and promising dreadful punishments to any who dared to continue.

So now the poachers who knew how to track moongliders simply followed a colony, waiting and hoping to find an elderly, sick or recently deceased moonglider, enabling them to get their hands on the precious wings legally. It was a distasteful and vulturous profession and those who practised it were looked down on by just about all other working class Elves. Fortunately for the moongliders very few fell ill, but all things age and die. The so called 'Carrion Elves' who waited for such deaths might spend many months at a time in the forests and have little respect from other Elves when they returned to civilization, but their trade was legal and a single pair of wings could easily net over a year's pay. Many Carrion Elves were very wealthy and master craftsmen would bargain with them long into the night over a newly 'procured' supply of wing material. It was all very unsavoury, but a part of Elysian life in the towns and villages of Elysia. The one good to come of it all was that a *gift* of moonglider craft was such a rare thing that the act had developed over the years so that anyone who received such a gift accepted it only as a token of true love.

These were the events that had been the cause of cloud-hoppers developing their bonding with moongliders and so one species could sense when the other was near.

Binnie took Bizarh almost straight to a moonglider colony, several miles back into the greenwood. The dragon could not help but spot them as he drew nearer, their shine iridescent in the afternoon sun. Binnie had to hover above the green canopy while Bizarh crashed through it to land a short distance from the sleeping creatures, before she came humming down through the hole he'd made to alight rather more delicately among the ferns beside him.

"We can rest now," she said, adding "if you like" as an afterthought. He was still after all a fire breathing giant and she didn't want him to think he was being bossed about.

But Bizarh just saw the wiseness of the remark.

"Yes. They won't awake until nightfall and we've put in quite a few miles today. I think a nap is a good idea."

Binnie just nodded in agreement.

Bizarh stamped the foliage around him flat then coiled, folding in his wings and gathering his tail about him before lowering his neck and head to the ground, tight in alongside his body. A great wriggle and he settled, closing his crystalline eyes. Then Binnie, in a simple gesture of trust, joined him and nestled against the warm edge of the scaly body. She too closed her eyes, but sleep did not come easily to either creature as the worry of the creeping brownness only a few miles away continuously invaded their thoughts.

Binnie
PHOEBE MOON © 2000

2

At Unicorn Glade

With the descending of dusk and the creeping advance of the night, Bizarh watched in silent fascination as the cluster of moongliders in the tree before him came awake. The iridescence of their wings seemed to die as the creatures themselves came to life, the last light of the day leaving a final glitter on the membranes.

Little Binnie watched with impatience, not appreciating the drama of transcendence from light into dark. She had seen this scene countless times before. In just a few more minutes it was almost pitch dark beneath the forest canopy and Bizarh had to strain his eyes to see. The moongliders, now stirring, stretched then began to move, slowly at first, from branch to branch checking the alertness of their family members and friends.

As if they were one, the night dwellers seemed to suddenly spot the big dragon looking intently on from beneath them, screeched a chorused warning and beat a hastily retreat to the topmost branches.

"Silly moongliders!" said Binnie quietly to herself, although Bizarh heard her clearly enough and couldn't help smiling to himself. With a deft spring she hummed into the night air and flew deftly up through the branches to calm the moongliders. To Bizarh's surprise several other cloud-hoppers seemed to suddenly appear from nowhere out of the greenery around him and also rose up into the tree tops. He hadn't even known they were about.

He waited patiently, aware of the bustle above him more through sound than by sight, and several long minutes passed before a small number of moongliders, each twinned with a cloud-hopper, came floating slowly down and settled tentatively on the ground a safe distance away from the big dragon.

In a clear show of both bravado in the face of her peers, and as proof of their safety in the presence of the green giant, Binnie left the group and flew straight across to Bizarh, landing between his front feet then turning to face her small friends with a 'there you are' expression on her face.

"See, it's perfectly safe," she said. "This is him, Bizarh."

There were several nods then, but the little group still took its own time to advance in greeting of the dragon. No one seemed in a hurry to come directly under the giant creature's glare.

"Good evening," said Bizarh rather cordially, bringing his head down almost to ground level to view the night dwellers at their own level.

There were several more nods and polite coughs by way of reply.

"Please forgive them," said Binnie, more than a hint of exasperation in her voice. "They're rather timid. It takes a little while for them to get used to a new face."

Her boldness now was in complete contrast to her own trepidation not a day earlier. Bizarh felt it prudent not to point this out at this time so he just nodded sagely before returning his attention to the group before him.

"Binnie has brought me a great distance to see you, concerning the strange brown stain upon the land," he said quietly.

This remark brought immediate reaction from the huddle of moongliders. They nodded vigorously and got quite animated, several of them beating their wings hard enough to momentarily lift off the ground.

"Yes, yes," several of them squeaked. It was the first time Bizarh had actually heard a moonglider speak and their high pitched tone surprised him. A pleasant surprise though, their voices not at all piercing, rather more tinkly, almost like the sound of children's laughter.

"Tell me," he found it hard to hide his smile. "What do you think it is?"

"It is creeping death!" came one voice.

"It doesn't stop!" came another.

"It's terrible!" a third.

Bizarh had trouble keeping track of who was saying what.

" I think it best if we just have one spokesperson," he suggested.

There were several more nods at the wise words, then a very long pause before a single moonglider plucked up courage and gingerly stepped forward. Recognizing him Binnie skipped out from beneath Bizarh's bulk and went to join her counterpart, escorting him forward until the pair stood squarely before the massive head of the green dragon. The moonglider shuffled uncomfortably from one pair of feet to the other. Binnie nudged him with her shoulder.

"Well go on. Introduce yourself."

"I... I'm... er... my name is Mira."

"And a good evening to you, Mira," breathed Bizarh softly. "Nice name," he added, trying to be as disarming as possible, but undoing much of the effort unintentionally by offering one of his fanged grins. He saw the sudden fear in the moonglider's eyes and felt it best to retreat slightly. He drew back his head, his neck coiling up over his back, creating a space between them.

"Tell me what you know."

"Well, it... it kills everything," squeaked Mira.

"We know that," interrupted Binnie, exasperated.

"Ssh!" hissed Bizarh. "I'm sure Mira is doing his best." Binnie looked suitably reproachful, which seemed somehow to bolster Mira's confidence. "Go on."

"It... it was a spell of sorts." The moonglider was no longer fretting. "Or rather, more than one spell. We all saw them crash together in the sky then fall to earth. Since then it's just been spreading. It kills everything in its path. And not just the plants either. Any forest creatures that are too small or too slow to get out of its way perish too!"

A surprised look had spread across Bizarh's face, which Mira thought was at the news of the creeping death.

"You say you actually saw it?" Bizarh asked, astounded. He wasn't all that clever he knew, but it was common knowledge that only wizards could see magic. Well, not so, it now appeared.

"Yes. And we watch it as it spreads. Even now, look." Mira turned to face where everyone knew the edge of the creeping brownness was, every other head turning to look with him. All the other moongliders nodded again but a frown burrowed Bizarh's brow. He couldn't see a thing.

"That's all very well." He shrugged, staring blindly into the dark. "But what can be done about it, that's what I'd like to know?"

When he turned back to look at the little group before him he found them all staring up at him in dismay.

"That's what we thought you would know," said Mira quietly.

"Oh."

"You can help, can't you?" asked several moongliders at once.

"Er... just give me a little while." Bizarh tried not to sound as baffled as he felt. "I'm sure I'll think of something."

But just how can I help he thought to himself, sitting absently back onto his haunches and leaning back against a tree which immediately bent to a very precarious angle. He seemed not to notice as he lapsed into deep thought, those watching him also falling silent.

Come to Unicorn Glade

"What?! Who said that?" Bizarh started.

"Said what?" asked Binnie.

Come to Unicorn Glade

"That voice. Didn't you hear it?"

All the cloud-hoppers and moongliders shook their heads in unison. Bizarh put his front paws over his ears and screwed his eyes tight shut. The silence was deafening as he held his breath. Then he heard it again and knew without understanding that the voice was somehow inside his head.

Come to Unicorn Glade

It was indeed inside his head. And he didn't like it one bit. Still, the message itself was clear enough and instinct told him that it was a message to be obeyed. He waited for a while but no more sounds came. All the while Binnie, Mira and the rest of the little group looked on in silent confusion.

Finally Bizarh looked down on them all and gave what he thought was a confident grin.

"I have decided to go to Unicorn Glade," he said firmly. "I've a feeling there is someone there who can help. Binnie, would you join me, and Mira too if that's all right? It might be helpful to have someone there who was right on the spot as it were." He wasn't quite sure why he'd added the last sentence, but some sudden instinct from deep within him pushed the words out.

Binnie nodded, but Mira looked decidedly frightened by the idea. The little cloud-hopper leaned in close to her partner.

"Have you ever flown on the back of a dragon?" she asked quietly.

"Of course not," replied Mira. "No one has."

"Well I have," said Binnie proudly. "On the back of my friend Bizarh here. And he's offering you the chance to do the same."

"I... I..." Mira looked up into the face of the green giant. He thought Bizarh was grinning just to be friendly, not realizing that dragons have very acute hearing and Bizarh smiled because he'd heard Binnie call him her friend.

"It is all to help stop the creeping brown death," added the cloud-hopper. At that Bizarh nodded in agreement.

Mira finally nodded too.

"That's settled then," said Bizarh, bringing himself back upright, and on a purely plant level the tree he'd been leaning against sprung back to its normal, vertical position and heaved a sigh of relief. "I'm going to get some sleep now, got a long flight in the morning. So just make sure you are ready my little friends, we leave just before first light."

Everyone nodded one final time, signalling the end of the meeting. All the moongliders lifted off, heading back into the branches while the cloud-hoppers dispersed back into the nearby forest, gone from sight in moments.

Little Binnie rejoined Bizarh, craning her neck to look up at him.

"Did you really hear a voice?" she asked.

"Yes. I don't know how or why it happened, but it was a really powerful call. And don't ask me how, but I'm also sure that I wasn't the only one to hear that call."

Around and through the hinterland of the great forests of Elysia, where almost all the various Elfin peoples live, criss-cross the roads, tracks, highways and byways that are the lifelines between all the villages. Like a huge, tangled spider's web all these roads eventually lead to a central hub. The great walled town of Talla-Weyre. And in the centre of this town within walls of its own sits a sprawling, rather squat and thick walled castle. A special castle, special for two reasons.

Firstly, and perhaps most importantly for the inhabitants of not just the town but the whole of Elysia, it is both the seat of power and home to their great and revered majesties the King and Queen.

Secondly though, it is a special place because living within its walls are not just one or even two, but no less than FOUR dragons of stature! Now, two of these dragons are permanent companions to their counterparts, the King and Queen, more of which later.

But the other two, each holding special places of trust within the castle have just, like Bizarh, sprung to alertness because they too have heard the call.

Come to Unicorn glade

"Hallo?"

Blairoggin heard the voice but could not locate its owner. He scanned the semi-darkness around him, the blackness not an obstacle to his view.

Living in the lower levels of the castle suited him. His eyesight, although perfectly normal in daylight, really came into its own at dusk and on into the dark. For his vision was enhanced with the unusual gift of being able to interpret not only the spectrum of normal light, from violet down to red, but further on down into the infra red. He in effect had heat sensitive eyes and could to all intents and purposes see perfectly well in the dark. This gift made him extremely well suited to his given task. The task of checking all the locks, clasps, bars, bolts and closures throughout the castle which made it a secure, safe place. A task usually done last thing at night and shortly before the dawn, hence his beneficial night vision. It was a task given to him by the King personally, a symbol of his highness's trust in the reliability and integrity of the dragon. A task the dragon was proud to carry out and for which he had over time become known across the land and much respected for. After all, what higher compliment could a King pay to one of his subjects than to entrust to that subject his personal safety?

Although very few outside Talla-Weyre had seen him in person the dark blue dragon was known by reputation to all. Blairoggin was the Keeper of the Keys.

Come to Unicorn Glade

Blairoggin didn't bother to speak again and it wasn't just because he was by nature a dragon of few words. He knew there was no one in the chamber with him. No heat signature, no movement and no echo in the sound of the voice. It wasn't in the chamber, it was in him!

He realized with some amazement that it must be some sort of telepathy. He had never before experienced anything like it, but knew that it was indeed possible. Over his years as Keeper of the Keys he had witnessed many strange visitors to the castle. Some on pilgrimage, some on the King's business and others just simply coming to see. Blairoggin was a wise dragon and kept his ears open and his mouth shut. He had heard much and even on occasion seen astounding things. Wizards in particular most impressed him. And so he was not shocked or too deeply disturbed by this sudden invasion of his thoughts. He sat back in the half-dark to contemplate the revelation, closing his eyes and trying to grasp some additional meaning from the few words. He was rewarded with a third call.

Come to Unicorn Glade

The message was undeniably clear and no doubt of great importance to have been aimed at him. He was amazed to find himself almost compelled to go. His curiosity burned bright at this sudden mystery, but his deep rooted sense of responsibility pulled at his conscience. Cocking his head to one side Blairoggin weighed up the dilemma.

The kingdom was quiet and at peace. As far as was known no

strife was apparent anywhere. All in the royal castle were loyal to the King, as indeed were the people of Talla-Weyre. His highness was in safe hands. Besides, Blairoggin knew well enough where Unicorn Glade was and if he left after unlocking at dawn he could be there and back without even being missed. Especially if he used the vertical exit. The dragon lifted easily to his feet and moved unerringly through the dark chambers beneath the castle until he reached the up draught chute. It was actually a huge chimney which allowed fresh air to circulate throughout the lower levels of the castle. The whole place was actually very well designed although this was the last thing on Blairoggin's mind now. He stepped beneath the open mouth of the air vent and gazed straight up the stone funnel at the few stars visible beyond its mouth.

He allowed a smile to split his normally sombre features. It was his secret. As far as he knew no one was aware that he could leave the castle unseen from the lower levels. He had discovered several years earlier that if he flew straight up the steadily narrowing chimney with enough speed, and folded his wings flat against his sides at the right moment, he could just fit through the mouth of the air vent and shoot out like a cork from a bottle, straight up into the air. A few hard beats and he was into the clouds and gone from sight. True, he had to return normally by flying in over the castle walls but no one could figure out how he had left in the first place. And as he was Blairoggin, Keeper of the Keys, no one dared to ask him.

Yes, at break of dawn one of the Kings most trusted dragons would leave his post and go in search of the sender of the call.

Up the wide cobbled roadway that approached the main castle gate stamped an Elf. A furious, red faced Elf!

He had a grievance. A serious grievance in his opinion and if he couldn't get satisfaction from the local province constable he'd jolly well go over the idiot's head. His superior, the Overseer, resided within the castle walls. He would see things right and if not, well by thunder, he would see the King himself!

Admittedly, it had taken several flagons of elven-grog to bring the

own level. The terrified soul was now suspended from the dragon's gleaming blade by his coat front, eye to eye with the beast some fifteen feet above the cobbles.

Decorum fixed him with a hard stare.

"You don't really think the King wants to see you, eh?" he hissed.

The Elf just shook his head. This close, the smell of pumice and sulphur made his eyes water. By the same token, to Decorum the smell of elven-grog was now quite intense.

"You don't really need to see the King, do you?"

A second, more emphatic shake of the head.

"You really just want to go home and sleep it off, don't you?"

This received an extremely vigorous nodding of the head.

"That's what I thought." Decorum turned his own head sideways and moved in close until the Elf's vision was completely filled with one huge crystalline eye, focused solely on him. "And if I see you here again without either an appointment or better manners, the next time you leave this gate will be as a small sack of warm cinders. Do I make myself clear?"

The Elf nodded so hard his neck hurt.

" Good. Then be on your way."

Decorum simply retracted his blades and the Elf, his means of support gone, dropped painfully onto his backside on the cobbles below. Even so he was on his feet in an instant and dashing off down the roadway as if the hounds of Hell were at his heels. All to loud cheers and jeers from the spectators.

"And change your breeches when you get home," the dragon called after the fleeing man. "You don't smell so good."

This raised an even louder roar of laughter from the crowd.

Decorum managed to keep his own laughter in until he had reached the sanctum of his guard house.

"There's one born every day," he chuckled. "And each day a surprise. I wonder what will happen next?"

Come to Unicorn Glade

"Eh? Who said that? Come out wherever you are, I can hear you!"

He looked about but saw no one. Poking his head out into the street revealed him to be totally alone.

"What's going on here?"

Come to Unicorn Glade

The voice came from within, not without. A message sent by magic. But by whom? And how dare they go inside his head without permission. Such an invasion of privacy. It was intolerable!

Come to Unicorn Glade

"All right, all right!" he shouted. "I'll come. But when I get there you'd better have a damn good explanation or you'll have me to reckon with!"

He hunkered down into a sullen silence, waiting for a reply.

But all he heard from then on was a deafening silence.

* * * * *

Every sentient animal in this part of Elysia knew where Unicorn Glade was and most knew how to get there.

But not so the bi-peds. For some time now the Elfin races, some of the forest faeries and even a few of the wizards had begun turning to the new fangled studies of something called 'science' when it came to maintaining their personal health.

The animals however remained faithful to the tried and tested ways of natural medicines, strong magic, aura energy and most of all the remedial powers of the forest mystics. And at Unicorn Glade lived one of the best. Her reputation was legendary even if little was known about her actual self.

Niaouli the Healer lived at the edge of Unicorn Glade. She had no apparent means of support and as far as was known was not a wizard either so exactly how she kept body and soul together was a mystery. But she still managed to do it with some style, which meant gossip and rumour about her was rife, because no one could deny that her castle was built to a very good standard. It was almost small enough to be called a manor but still had several elegant slim towers with needle pointed spire roofs. Like the rest of the building they were neat, showed excellent quality of build and quietly shouted of taste, the whole castle an eye-pleasing picture of symmetry and balance. There were many Elfin barons and even a few wizards who could learn much simply from looking at Niaouli's castle. Even its position within Unicorn Glade was somehow discreet and unassuming. It did not encroach on the beauty of the area yet did not detract from or try to hide its own beauty, sited as it was up against the pine woods at one end of the glade. It made a tactful and enhancing addition to the overall scene that was Unicorn Glade.

With the heady, scented pines to one side and the fire-flare trees opposite, each tall, leafy boundary formed part of a living frame surrounding a lush open stretch of meadow with a softly whispering, clear, sparkling stream bisecting the greenness. The glade was a true picture of natural beauty, the only slightly deceptive thing about it being its name.

Unicorns did in all honesty gather here a few times each year, but these events were only ever witnessed by a privileged few. And it was true that the occasional elder Unicorn did fly unexpectedly in to graze upon the rich, sweet greenery, but for most of the time Unicorn Glade was glaringly devoid of actual Unicorns.

Today however, was something of a special day. A very special day.

There were indeed several Unicorns in the glade, but they were not grazing. They were simply waiting. And at their head, standing quiet and still was a very special Unicorn.

Only the elder, mature Unicorns could actually fly and this particular creature, by dint of the great span of her wings and the huge number of spiral turns in her horn (which as everyone knows is the true way to tell the age of a Unicorn) could mean only one thing.

It was Crystal. The oldest, wisest, most beautiful and virtually never seen of her race. Her shyness was almost as well known as her wisdom. Yet here she was in plain sight and waiting for something. Or someone.

They had not been waiting all that long and it was just after the sun had reached its zenith when she casually raised her eyes to the sky as the first dragon came in. She had somehow felt his approach. The first the younger Unicorns knew of it was as they were momentarily blacked out as the dark shadow of the creature swept over them, blinking the sunlight briefly off then on again. The silhouette flowed across the greenness of the open meadow before merging with the darkness beneath the trees opposite.

Blairoggin had kept low, hugging the tree tops for the duration of his flight, a combination of his dislike of the bright sunlight and his natural tendency towards stealth making him hug the contours of the land. He swept by once more, wheeled away in a steep turn making him appear to pivot on one wing tip and offering a brief but spectacular view of his great wingspan, then descended smoothly to land lightly on the far side of the meadow, away from Crystal, the other Unicorns and Niaouli's castle. After scanning the whole glade carefully he nodded a brief acknowledgement to Crystal then carefully backed into the fire-flame trees and settled down in a great coil among the shadow and shade there. Not a word had been said. And the waiting continued.

In complete contrast to the arrival of the Keeper of the Keys, Decorum approached straight out of the sun. A fast moving dark shape high up in the blueness of the sky, his approach was witnessed by one and all, as was his intention, with wings partially retracted so that they resembled the delta shape of the tail end of an arrow's fletching. This dart-like backward sweep of the wings disrupted the airflow across the trailing edge of the wing surface and the result of this trick he had learned long ago was to cause a great whooshing sound as he cut through the air. The faster the speed the louder the sound. With a roar he flashed over the waiting throng, executed an extremely skilful stall turn above the far end of the Glade and darted back in, landing with an aggressive, ground jarring thud right at the head of the Unicorn herd. He was still folding his wings in as he spoke.

"Right then!" he said bluntly to Crystal. "What's all this about?

Why have I been summonsed and who's responsible for it all? Eh?"

The lesser Unicorns looked visibly shocked at this bold effrontery to one as great as Crystal but she just smiled a charming, utterly disarming and to Decorum a rather disconcerting smile. He drew his neck back in surprise at the effect it had on him.

"Be patient, my brave dragon," she said softly. "All will become apparent soon enough. But not until everyone is here."

"But..."

"If you would just wait? Please?" Her voice was as soft as down, calming and delivered from a face of such beauty that Decorum chose simply not to reply rather than just blub incoherently. He had never been so effectively calmed, controlled and at the same time unnerved before. But he was not without his dignity and so gave the Unicorn a tightly controlled bow of the head combined with his best 'I do this only under sufferance' stare as his acceptance of her request.

Crystal beamed a beautiful smile of gratitude while behind her a few of the young Unicorns began to giggle at the sight of a great and fierce dragon bowing down to the much smaller, white winged horse. This merriment stopped immediately when Decorum shot them a withering, hard-eyed stare. He might have been cut short by Crystal but he would most certainly not endure being laughed at. The fierceness of his look caused several of the young Unicorns to hide behind the bigger animals.

"Good enough," he growled under his breath, but just loud enough to be heard, and with a last nod to Crystal turned his back on the herd and walked away. Only then did he catch sight of Blairoggin, barely visible in the dappled shade of the trees. They naturally recognised each other and the Gate Keeper nodded, received one in return, then moved across to the same tree line. Making sure to give the Keeper of the Keys enough room and an uninterrupted view of the glade, he settled down himself, this time in the bright sun. And the waiting continued.

The sun was much lower, almost touching the tops of the trees, when the third dragon appeared. Flying low and steady his approach attracted everyone's attention for two reasons. As if it were not surprise enough that this unknown dragon was emerald green in colour, it also carried something, or someone, on its back.

Bizarh swept around in a wide, gentle arc and came in long and low from the far end of the Glade like a swan about to land on a lake. At the last moment he stalled his broad wings and landed as carefully as he could so as not to dislodge his passengers. Even so, a soft landing by Bizarh's standard was still considered more of a controlled crash by the spectators as they witnessed him gracefully pause just above the ground then thud earthward with an impact that left deep imprints of all his feet in the soil.

Then, watched in total silence by all the onlookers, a tiny cloud-hopper flitted down from his broad, scaly back and landed deftly on the turf before him. She paid no attention at all to the glittering moonglider that still slept soundly on top of the dragon, wings outstretched gathering the rays of the afternoon sun.

"Well, here we are," said Binnie. "Unicorn Glade. What happens next?"

"Beats me." Bizarh shrugged a great shrug that made his wing membranes rustle but still did nothing to disturb the moonglider's peaceful slumbers. "Perhaps she knows." He nodded towards the lead Unicorn.

"It's Crystal!" gasped Binnie in awe-struck recognition.

"Is that good?" asked Bizarh.

"Don't you know anything?" scolded the cloud-hopper. Bizarh just smiled at the little creature's bold brashness as she continued. "She knows everything. Some say she has magic powers. Others say she can see your future."

"Oh, *that* Crystal." The dragon nodded sagely, not believing these rumours for an instant.

Crystal stepped forward and nodded at the strange group.

"Welcome Bizarh, Binnie, and I do believe the little fellow on top is Mira."

Now Bizarh was impressed. "How did you..."

"Never mind now," came the soft, soothing reply. In a while all will become clear. But we must wait until the dusk. You have others of your kind over there." She nodded towards the fire-flame tree line. "Meet with them if you like, but there is one other person needed to complete the gathering and then all will be revealed. So you must wait a little while. Please?"

Bizarh looked across at the two dragons staring at him in open curiosity. Both he saw were dragons of stature. He'd heard of such dragons of course but had never actually seen one before, let alone two.

"I think I'll just wait," he mumbled and gave them a wide berth, settling down in a loose coil a short way away from them on the sunny side of the meadow, positioning himself to afford Mira the benefit of the last of the sun's rays.

Finally the sun sank below the tree line and the light began to fade. Mira began the first stirrings into wakefulness, still totally oblivious to just where he was or to the remarkable gathering of creatures around him, almost all of whom were pondering on what was to happen next.

Blairoggin was beginning to get anxious. Soon it would be fully dark and he would have to be back to secure the King's castle. Decorum drummed his front claws on the ground, his patience beginning to wear. Bizarh rested easily, a virtually motionless coil of emerald green scales. He had learned long ago how to wait, it was after all what happened most of the time in the deep forests. Little Binnie took up her now customary position in front of Bizarh's front paws. They were almost as big as she, but the figurehead position made her feel important and the green dragon felt no need to correct her on that rather grandiose assumption.

All the pondering stopped as every head turned to look in the direction of the tidy castle. A woman had suddenly appeared outside the gate and was now approaching.

It was apparent to all that she was a vision of loveliness, even at first glance. As she drew nearer this was confirmed, not just by her look, but also her demeanour. She was a feast for the eyes.

A cherubic face with glittering blue eyes set in clear skin was framed by a great flaxen mane of hair that flowed down over her shoulders and back almost to waist level, while its finer strands streamed out behind her into the scented evening air as she moved ever closer. She had Elfin features, but somehow didn't look quite Elfin. She was tall for a start, which no doubt helped the spreading rumour that she might be a wizard, but there was something odd, delightfully odd, about her. It was almost as if she'd had mixed parentage and gained the best of both from the union.

Elfin and faerie perhaps thought Bizarh.

The long, flowing, opaque robe that wasn't so much wrapped about her as shrouding her was made of some light, airy material and the green dragon decided that it must have contained a certain amount of spider webbing woven into it to move as it did. The apparently seamless garment reached fully to the ground and seemed to swirl about her as she moved, giving the impression that she didn't so much stride as almost float across the glade towards the now gaping onlookers.

Finally stopping alongside Crystal, who came as near to a curtsy as it is possible for a horse to do, the mystery woman simply beckoned with her soft, pale hands for the three dragons to come closer. Entranced by her beauty and serenity, they all walked eagerly forward until they were lined up before her, where they sat upright, three giant living gargoyles towering over her and the rest of the gathering. She craned her elegant neck back to smile up at them and they found themselves offering fang-filled grins in return.

Thank you.

They nodded as one, knowing the voice to be hers, before realising that her lips had not moved.

"What?" exploded Decorum, killing the solemnity of the moment stone dead.

Do not be afraid. I know you can hear, even though I do not speak. These are mindwords.

"Well that explains who called us here then," said Blairoggin sagely, not feeling it necessary to admit that he had never heard of mindwords before, but now knew well enough what words in his mind sounded like.

"Fair enough," said Bizarh, feeling he should join in. "But just why did you call us and who exactly are you?"

Forgive my rudeness. The woman bowed deeply to the dragon trio in apology, her hair making a delightful soft whooshing sound as it brushed over her flowing robe. Then she opened her arms wide.

I am Niaouli.

There were gasps from some of the young Unicorns.

And as for why you are all here, she continued, looking to Bizarh, *I think you already know, my beautiful green dragon.*

"He does?" asked Blairoggin and Decorum in unison.

"I do?" echoed Bizarh.

Niaouli did not answer, but simply faced the three dragons. This time she did not smile.

Close your eyes and I will show you all what has happened.

Without question the three closed their crystalline eyes and watched in amazement the pictures suddenly filling their minds.

They saw three separate spells roaring across the night sky, the blinding flash of their collision and the magi-welded tri-spell fall to earth. They heard the creatures of the deep forest cry out in pain and anguish for their home. And finally watched how the tri-spell fouled the green land and killed as it grew.

The images were gone just as suddenly as they came, but lingered in the mind like a bad taste in the mouth.

Blairoggin and Decorum opened their eyes and looked directly at the unknown green dragon for the first time.

" You have actually seen this?" asked the Keeper of the Keys slowly.

"Yes. And so have these two." Bizarh nodded down towards Binnie, still standing at his feet, but now joined by Mira. The little moonglider huddled close to the cloud-hopper trembling in fear and awe of all the great and wonderful creatures that surrounded him and were now looking at him.

And that is why you are here.

All eyes reverted to Niaouli. Apart from Blairoggin and Mira, who both had excellent night vision, everyone else was squinting to try and bring the Healer into focus. In the very last of the evening light she was now not much more than a ghostly blur in her gossamer gown.

Forgive me, she said apologetically as she realised their problem. *The darkness masks us from each other but it was necessary to wait until night, for the moongliders are the key to our problem.*

"We... we are?" It was the first time Mira had spoken and he could see Niaouli smile warmly at him even if the others couldn't. But she did not answer his question. Instead she spread her arms wide against the night and called out a name that no one knew. Three times she did this and as her cry faded away the air around those gathered began to hum softly. The castle dragons crouched, wary of the strange sound but Bizarh recognised the song. Glowbugs.

He had often watched in amusement on warm summer evenings as the luminous insects were chased by the mischievous little hushdragons that lived among the multicoloured crown flowers often found carpeting the forest floor. The whirling flashes of fluorescence created by the pursued bugs as they weaved and jinked to escape made for quite marvellous impromptu light shows.

The air around the group became thicker with the soft hum and as if to an unheard signal all the little insects lit up at once. Unseen in the darkness the night fliers had landed on everyone or else hung hovering in the air above them. The entire group was suddenly bathed in a soft iridescent amber glow.

"It's beautiful!" gasped one of the young Unicorns.

"Well, I can see all right now," acknowledged Bizarh.

"Huh! I feel like a street light," grunted Decorum, glancing down at his glowing body.

It will do, nodded Niaouli, turning again to Mira. *Yes my little moonglider, you are indeed the key, but these good dragons are the ones that would help turn that key.*

"How come they are so important then?" asked Blairoggin looking down at the timid creature that cowered under his sudden attention. It didn't look much like a key and he felt he should know, keys being his stock in trade after all.

Because they can see what we cannot.

Decorum was rapidly tiring of this cryptic game of words. He was an honest, straight talking dragon and expected those talking to him to reply in the same forthright manner.

"Well that's all well and good," he said gruffly. "But what do you want with the three of us. This green dragon here..."

"Bizarh," interrupted Bizarh.

"...has nothing better to do," Decorum continued as if he'd not heard. "But the rest of us have responsibilities to the King. We really must be going."

"That's right," agreed Blairoggin.

I know you have your duties, but let me show you what will happen if you do not heed my call. Although your King needs you, a higher power now needs you more.

"There is no higher power than the King!" said Decorum loudly. Proudly.

Elysia needs you. Niaouli's mindwords were quiet enough but filled with power.

There was a silence then, broken only by the soft humming of the glowbugs.

The Healer allowed some time for the magnitude of her words to sink in then gestured towards Crystal. The oldest of the Unicorns obediently moved closer.

This as you all know is the Unicorn of Unicorns. It is said that Crystal has second sight. Believe me now when I tell you that it is true. But know also that the future is not set in stone. It can be changed by those with determination enough to try. Yet if nothing comes of this meeting tonight, the future that Crystal sees, the future of Elysia itself, is no future at all.

Everyone close their eyes and I will let you all share her vision.

With that Niaouli watched as they all closed their eyes, then placed one palm flat onto Crystal's forehead. The other arm she thrust out, splayed fingers towards the gathered. Then she screwed her own eyes tight shut and began to concentrate.

And Crystal looked to the future.

A picture began to expand into the minds of those around the Healer and the Unicorn locked together in telepathic projection. A picture that at first was pleasing to the mind's eye.

The vast, rolling greenness of the forests of Elysia became visible, viewed from a vantage point high in the sky. Great rolling tracts of dense, virgin woodland, its more familiar fringe areas marked by rough roads and dotted here and there with small yet bustling villages. Far off in the hazy distance could be seen the outline of the city wall and the lifting skyline of Talla-Weyre. But there was no time to enjoy the sight as the viewers were dragged away from this marvellous vista and carried off far into the deep forest.

Suddenly there, way down below them, was an innocuous looking small circular patch of brownness. This was zoomed in on. Closer and closer until it was plain to see that within it all the plants, small creatures and even the soil itself was dead.

With that, and to the total astonishment of all who had never witnessed a future vision before, which after all is very few, time itself began to speed up.

The brownness expanded out like the first ripple from a stone thrown into the middle of a pond. Expanding out at an ever increasing rate and eating up the land, the plant life and all else before it. Whole woods withered and died. The forests withered and died. And the animals in those forests. Not just individual creatures, but whole species were consumed and destroyed. While all the time the brownness spread on out, ever faster. On beyond the confines of the now dead forests and out into the crop covered hinterlands. These crops too died and, suddenly poverty stricken, the Elfin villages that relied upon them suffered, rapidly fell prey to malnutrition and pestilence and the homes, huts and hovels became dens of disease.

Without the crops and the wealth, sustenance and good standard of living they provided, the people who could fled to the city, innocently bringing the disease with them. Talla-Weyre, once the jewel in Elysia's crown, rapidly fell into disarray, degenerating into a seething pit of squalor and misery. No one was spared. The good died as quickly, or worse as slowly, as the bad.

Even the Queen was struck down. Her subjects, despite their own suffering, wept for her, as did the King. But nothing could be done to save her or Talla-Weyre.

Or the people, the creatures or the forests.

Or Elysia.

Niaouli snatched her hand from Crystal's brow and slapped it to her own, shaking her head in disbelief. The Oldest of the Unicorns had a dirty look on her usually serene face, ashamed that she had shown such a thing to those about her. Some of the younger Unicorns were crying openly. Binnie and Mira hid their faces against Bizarh's giant paws. The three dragons sat in grim faced silence, shocked.

Niaouli took several deep breaths to try and regain her composure then looked slowly up into the sagging faces of the winged giants before her.

It can be changed, she said slowly and there was a pause before she added quietly, *I hope.*

Normally concerned only with his own interests and duties Decorum was surprised to suddenly find himself speaking for his fellow dragons as well as for himself. To their agreeing nods he said grimly.

"What must we do?"

"Mira"
Phoebe Moon
2000 ©

3
BIZARH TWIST

Before long the first part of Niaouli's rescue bid for the forests of Elysia had been arranged. Only the first part though for what happened after these things had been set in motion was anybody's guess. Even Crystal's mind's eye could not see towards the outcome, there were so many twists and turns in the unknown path that lay ahead.

But this first, important step on that tortuous path was that all three dragons should return to the advancing edge of the creeping brownness to witness the evil first hand but, more importantly, to collect a moonglider each.

"Why do we need a moonglider?" asked Blairoggin.

Because they can see what we cannot, Niaouli repeated. *It is common enough knowledge that wizards leave their own auras on a spell when it is created by them, yes?*

Everyone nodded, fully aware that wizards often took great pains to point this out.

And it is also common knowledge that only the wizards themselves can see these auras, right?

And that was the reason wizards pointed out this fact. It highlighted their own importance.

Yet at this second observation all but Mira nodded.

Wrong! These little moongliders... she nodded down at Mira and he shyly smiled back up at the beautiful woman, unexplainably grateful that she now lavished her full attention, no matter how briefly, on him... *have a special vision which allows them also to witness these auras.*

Now everyone's attention focused on Mira and his warm gratitude turned to chill intimidation. He found himself huddling tight up against Bizarh's scaly bulk for protection.

I see you all understand now. A half smile crossed Niaouli's cherubic face. *We must seek out these wizards who cast the spells that combined to create this menace.*

"Three," piped up Mira despite his fear.

Yes, three, agreed Niaouli as if she didn't already know how many, although just how she knew remained a mystery. *And that is why I have summoned you three dragons, because there are possibly great distances to be travelled in search of them. Clearly the little moongliders cannot fly so far, but they are our eyes to find what we cannot see. And so you must each have a moonglider to guide you. To see the right wizards by their aura.*

"And they're to ride on our backs?" asked Decorum rather incredulously.

"It's not so bad," said Bizarh, unaware that he had already broken the unwritten dragon rule that dragons, or at least dragons of stature, always flew alone. "They don't weigh you down at all, you just have to be a bit careful not to do any sharp manoeuvres and accidentally tip them off."

"Huh!" grunted the Gate Keeper, unimpressed that any dragon of stature would condescend to let anything ride on his back. But he was not one to shirk from a challenge. "OK, but why a cloud-hopper too?"

"Because they go with the moonglider," said Little Binnie sharply before remembering just who had asked the question. She darted behind one of Bizarh's paws as Decorum shot her a fierce stare.

Blairoggin interjected before Decorum said or did something rash.

"Well I suppose the castle and His Royal Highness will have to manage without us for a while." He knew without doubt that what they had all been summoned for took precedence over all else, but his unhappiness at the difficult situation it put him in was clear in his voice. "I just hope he'll understand."

"True enough," agreed Decorum sourly. "But this creeping brownness has to be stopped."

There, he had finally said what everyone knew but had feared to say out loud. There was a heavy silence.

And I am sure that you are the dragons to stop it. Niaouli's mindwords cut the stillness, quiet yet reassuringly firm. She smiled up at the three dragons of stature assembled before her. *There are other great dragons within the kingdom, but you here are all honest, strong and true. The best.*

I just hope you are good enough. Her last thought was hers alone.

"We won't let you down," said Bizarh boldly as if in direct reply to her unheard concern. "Or Elysia."

"Huh. Hark at our new 'leader'," said Decorum sarcastically. "Well I hope he's not as green as he's coloured."

Now, no arguing. Niaouli smiled broadly then. *Once you have collected your passengers you must each go your own way, so there will be no leader. And who can say what lies ahead for each of you or indeed for any of us, but I do know that all here wish you the best of fortune and hope fervently for your success.*

"Here, here," said Crystal wholeheartedly.

"For Elysia and the King," said Blairoggin proudly.

"Elysia, and the King," echoed everyone else.

Thank you, my beautiful dragons. Now I bid you get some rest for at first light the adventure of adventures begins for you. She didn't feel the need to add that the future of Elysia rested with them too. She bowed deeply to the dragons.

With a flourish of their long necks the Keeper of the Keys, the Gate Keeper and the forest dragon all bowed low to the mysterious and beautiful Healer.

She accepted the accolade with a warm, charming smile, gestured with an acknowledging hand towards Crystal and the other silent Unicorns then without another mindword swept away from the gathered beasts and set off towards her castle.

All the glowbugs immediately followed after her, creating a glowing train that strung out behind her like the wake of a ship as she swept across the open darkness of Unicorn Glade.

Suddenly robbed of their light source the watching group were plunged into night, but it wasn't just the darkness that now pressed in on the three dragons, the Unicorns and Bizarh's little companions. Each was silently contemplating the full horror of what Crystal had shown would happen, if they were not successful in the gargantuan task that now lay ahead.

The three dragons flew out together next morning, a rare and quite spectacular sight. Bizarh led off in a very loose delta formation, the two castle dragons astern and off at either side. For a while the trailing pair couldn't help staring at the oddness of seeing a 'back packing' dragon.

Mira was of course asleep, wings spread flat against Bizarh's scaly back, soaking in the early morning light. Little Binnie had taken up her now customary position higher up between the green dragon's shoulders at the base of his long neck. Her growing flying experience told her the best way to push through the air stream was to cause as little drag as possible and adopt a streamlined 'attack' posture. She was now in her optimum flying position, laying low between Bizarh's slowly flexing shoulder blades, with her own wings folded straight back and snout pushed out directly into the airflow.

Blairoggin, who had on occasion travelled far across the inhabited areas of Elysia during his night forays, suddenly realised as he watched the little cloud-hopper that she closely resembled the figureheads of the wind driven trader ships that travelled the coastal waters of the King's domain. Their sculptured faces looking forward, ahead of the wind, leading the craft and her crew towards a new destination. He found himself smiling at the comparison.

Decorum entertained no such poetic thoughts. He was otherwise engaged, trying to mark his way as they flew above the trackless forest by noting any prominent or otherwise distinctive topographical land features he could see. But after miles of apparently endless green canopy one fire-flame grove looked very much like another and he gave up. It galled him to accept the fact that he must put his trust in an odd looking green coloured dragon he'd never met before, a dragon that in fact no one had ever seen before, and he wasn't even sure he liked. But he had to admit the lad certainly seemed to know exactly where he was heading, even if no one else did. Finally he resigned himself to it and glanced over at Blairoggin who nodded back as if in silent agreement to his unsaid thoughts. The two castle dragons simultaneously swooped in and closed up just behind Bizarh's wingtips. This allowed them to use the increase in the slipstream effect created by the lead dragon's flight for more efficient flying. In this much tighter formation they could make better time. They were becoming a team.

And all the while the forest flashed past beneath them, as if it were itself fleeing rearward and the flyers above it standing still, its passing pushing the dragon trio further and further away from civilised Elysia and into the darkest and impenetrable wild woods.

Until they came upon the brownness.

All three spotted the discolouration at the same time. Blairoggin and Decorum were at once filled with a burning curiosity, but Bizarh just felt a dreadful realisation, knowing without hesitation that he had not flown back as far as he had flown out. The creeping destruction was indeed spreading, now even more rapidly.

They swooped down and Bizarh led them out over the stain upon the earth for a few silent minutes to let the others have a good look at what the spreading tri-spell did, before eventually wheeling away to look for a shimmering tree.

It didn't take too long and Bizarh, not wishing to disturb anyone's slumbers, landed a short distance away in his usual heavy footed manner. The castle dragons circled for a minute longer trying to find a suitable landing spot, but with the complete absence of any gaps within the woodland canopy were forced to adopt the green dragon's apparently ungainly and amateurish landing style. They too finally dropped straight down through the greenery to thud heavily to the ground. Not pretty but undoubtedly effective and they both came to the same conclusion at the same time that perhaps Bizarh wasn't quite as ignorant as he had first appeared.

The three were met shortly after by a delegation of cloud-hoppers, which stayed back from the overpowering sight of three huge dragons. Their fears were soon dispelled by little Binnie who had hummed forward to meet them and explain that the great beasts were here to help.

While being led through the broad, towering trunks to the moonglider roost Blairoggin moved alongside Bizarh, who he noticed appeared immediately at home within the greenwood. The Keeper of the Keys had only ever seen dragons of stature in the towns, or at least always in the company of people. He had to admit though that the forests of Elysia suited Bizarh, or was it the other way around?

"Just how long has this damage to the forest been going on?" he asked. "I must admit it quite stunned me when I first saw it. I didn't really believe it could be quite as bad as Crystal had foretold but... well, I mean. Just completely dead! Not a single blade of green grass or a solitary ground crawler."

"That's just how I felt when I first laid eyes on it." Bizarh nodded in understanding. "As far as I know it's only been here a few days. And I'll tell you something else. First time up I could fly right around the patch of brownness in a few minutes, but just now we were over it for at least as long as that and never reached the other side. I think it is spreading out at an increasing rate."

Decorum, who did seem to have the knack of stating the obvious, had been listening from behind them.

"So, it could all unfold just as Crystal showed us then."

He too had not really fully believed the Unicorn. But now, having seen it with his own eyes, he at last grasped just what was at stake and how he and his fellow dragons were now entwined within it.

"Looks like it," said Bizarh and Blairoggin together.

There was nothing more to be said after that.

The strange troupe reached the moonglider roost, finding a cluster of cloud-hoppers gathered below it. Bizarh allowed the other two dragons a few awe filled moments' view of the sparkling, iridescent beauty of the sight before getting on with the business in hand.

Decorum and Blairoggin found it hard to drag their eyes from such a sight as was never before seen up close by any city dweller and were quite amazed at the apparent nonchalance displayed by the green dragon and his little friend who were carrying on as if nothing could have been more ordinary. Perhaps it was an everyday sight within the deep forests of Elysia? But what a sight!

Bizarh had halted his companions short of the actual roost and went forward with Binnie, bringing his head down almost to ground level to be at the same eye level as the small band of cloud-hoppers he now faced. They were familiar enough with Bizarh, at least by reputation even if not having met him before in person, but were clearly nervous of the two strange dragons and there were several timorous glances in their direction.

"It's all right," Bizarh explained. "These are the two who will carry those who would help us find the wizards responsible for the creeping brownness. To make it stop. And I'm sure you must know by now that we must find three in all."

There was a chorus of nods at that.

"Little Binnie and Mira have already agreed to join with me but two more pairs will have to go too, each pair with one of these castle dragons." He cocked his head in the direction of the watching pair. The looks of uncertainty on the cloud-hoppers' faces said it all. "Believe me when I tell you that they are both brave and true despite their size or manner. After all, they are in the service of the King himself and were chosen above all others by Niaouli the Healer. What more proof do you need?"

There were several nods of agreement then. Bizarh briefly wondered if out here it was the mention of the King's name or Niaouli's which carried more weight, but he could tell they were coming around. A little more and they would be convinced and agree to join the great adventure. At that moment Binnie spoke up in support of her huge friend.

"These are all good dragons," she said emphatically then, in a show of confidence hummed up into the air and landed lightly on top of Bizarh's head, perching rather precariously on the smooth scales there, her hooves close together between the green dragon's stubby horns. “And they are brave enough to try and fight the creeping death. To do that the wizards must be found and that means long travel. The castle dragons are offering to do that, but it means nothing if we and the moongliders do not go too. So we must also be brave. These good dragons will take care of us and together we can unite and try to stop the spreading death.”

It was a tremendous speech from a creature who just days before was so timid as to hide from the dragon she now stood upon and the open mouthed silence from all the watching cloud-hoppers said more than words ever could. Bizarh was so proud of his little friend then.

“Well said,” whispered Bizarh and nodded his head in agreement, careful though not to inadvertently dislodge the orator from her lofty position.

“Yes.” Blairoggin’s quietly powerful voice next caught the little group’s attention. “We want to help and together I am sure we really can make a difference.”

“Right!” Decorum had no intention of being left out. “So stop messing about. We can do it!”

The Gate Keeper’s rather forthright approach was perhaps a bit strong for the timid cloud-hoppers, but his firm commitment and determination to their task came across well enough.

“True words.” Bizarh kept still as Little Binnie took off, flew into his view and landed right before the other cloud-hoppers. She adopted what was for a cloud-hopper a bold, wide-legged stance and the tilt of her head said ‘there you are, told you so’.

“We,” she looked over her shoulder to indicate the two castle dragons, “need a moonglider and cloud-hopper pair to partner each of these true dragons. You know why and just what is at stake. What say you all?”

There were low mutterings from the cloud-hoppers. Binnie turned back to Bizarh.

“Let them talk it over,” she said. “It’ll take a little while for them to decide. You must understand that the cloud-hoppers who agree speak not only for themselves but also for their moonglider partner.

But they'll do the right thing, you'll see."

Bizarh gave her a reassuring wink then moved back to join the other dragons. They had heard and understood. The three watched in silence as the group opposite them sank into a deep and animated discussion.

The decision to go didn't in itself take too long. The bulk of the clearly urgent discussions was in persuading rather than choosing just who should 'volunteer' to join the dragons. Plus, with only the moongliders able to see wizards' auras it came down to which of the gossamer winged creatures had the most stable temperaments and would not too readily balk at being a passenger on some huge and unknown dragon. It was quite fortunate then that once a cloud-hopper and moonglider paired they were partners for life and well knew their opposite number's character. It was to outsiders a strange arrangement, but the creatures simply needed each other. Neither was a part of the other's family group but more of a best friend, one always had to look out for and support the other, their bonding seeming to be on some unknown, spiritual level.

Finally the tight cluster turned as one to face the three dragons. Little Binnie skipped forward to join them and after a few brief words she returned, leading the two slightly hesitant cloud-hoppers that had reluctantly detached themselves from the rest. As they drew closer Bizarh's extra sensitive hearing picked up Binnie's whispers.

"Blairoggin, that's the very dark blue one, doesn't say much but when he speaks it's worth listening to. Decorum, the light coloured one, is more aggressive, but his bark is much worse than his bite. They're both all right. Honest."

Bizarh had to hide a smile and looked solemnly on as the little trio came to a halt beneath the gaze of the dragons. They arched their necks to look up at the huge beasts.

"Here they are." Binnie's voice was now loud and almost too chirpy. She turned her attention to her companions. "Make your choice."

Neither moved nor spoke. Both seemed at that moment rooted to the spot.

Blairoggin decided to take the initiative, lowered his head to almost ground level, turned to one side and focused one crystalline eye on the cloud-hopper nearest him.

"You must be very brave to want to ride with us." His normally powerful voice was soft. Empathic. "I would be proud to have you ride along with me."

The cloud-hopper in question was momentarily lost for words, her fear briefly gone, smothered by a sudden total fascination with the workings of the dragon's eye she was now close enough to see her reflection in. The hard looking lens flexed like a wing membrane as it focused and the creature being inspected wondered just what was really being seen through that marvel of nature.

Her recovery came quickly as she realised she was staring, which of course is rather rude.

"Er... er... my... my name is Kizzy. I... I..."

"Hello Kizzy. I'm very pleased to meet you."

Kizzy nodded, a nod deep enough to almost become a curtsy.

"Why don't you fly up onto my back." Blairoggin's suggestion was still delivered in his soft, pacifying tone. "Just to see if you like it. You'll probably have a much better view from up there too."

"Oh... ok." Kizzy wouldn't dare to offend by refusing and immediately flexed her wings then hummed up into the air, skirting the huge head before flitting up over his bulk and alighting on his broad back as gently as she could, as if afraid that her touchdown might in some way hurt him.

"There. Not so bad, eh?" Blairoggin's head swept up and he twisted his neck until he was once again eyeing his little passenger.

"No... no actually. I... er... it's quite high isn't it? And yes you're right, I do have a better view."

"Well there you are." There was a moment's silence then together their heads turned to look down on the solitary cloud-hopper below them on the ground. Binnie had already hummed up onto Bizarh in a show of cloud-hopper solidarity.

"Not so bad," she echoed.

The grounded cloud-hopper just looked sheepishly up at 'her' dragon.

Decorum gave the tiny thing only a moment then just flicked his head.

"Well, come on," he said briskly. "Get up here!"

The little creature visibly blanched, but didn't dare hesitate and chance sampling the giant dragon's wrath. Without a word she instantly lifted into the air and flew straight up onto Decorum's back, watched every inch of the way by the Gate Keeper. No sooner had the cloud-hopper touched down on the blue scales than Decorum's head was inches from her own. Close enough for his breath to stir her fur as he spoke, his voice suddenly so low that only she could hear it.

"Don't worry little one," he whispered. "I will take good care of you, on my honour, yes?"

The startled cloud-hopper could only nod.

"Decorum!" the dragon then said loudly and abruptly. "That's my name. And you are?"

"Zoozie." The word was out before Zoozie even realised.

"All right Zoozie." Her new 'partner' nodded briefly. "The others can sit around and wait all day for the moongliders to wake up if they like but I think we can do better than that. Let's fly, eh? Hang on!"

And with that the light blue dragon half coiled and launched, the down draught from his wings making the other unprepared, still silently spectating cloud-hoppers turn away from the blast. Going almost vertically up with a shocked and wide-eyed looking Zoozie working hard to stay on, the Gate Keeper whooshed out through the gap in the canopy through which the sun shone down onto the moonglider roost. He banked left, almost immediately gone from sight. Only Bizarh, who with his past experience of flying with a passenger, recognised the control and care with which the Gate Keeper executed the manoeuvre as the new pair wheeled away. Decorum was being careful, in his own brusque way.

"They'll be all right," he said confidently. "In fact Blairoggin, it might be a good idea for you and your new friend to get in some practice too. There's a bit of a knack to it. Besides, he's right. It'll be a few hours before the sun sets and you can pick up your other passengers."

The Keeper of the Keys simply nodded his agreement to the wise words.

"C'mon Kizzy." He smiled then turned his eyes to the small patch of blue sky above them. "This is going to be fun. Trust me."

Kizzy didn't look quite so sure and hung on grimly as the dragon lifted effortlessly off and disappeared through the canopy.

* * * * *

By the time dusk had fallen the castle dragons were becoming more competent in the art of 'accompanied' flying and the cloud-hoppers had overcome most of their fear of flying at both speed and altitude. Like Little Binnie a few days earlier, they too had discovered the magnificent exhilaration to be had from riding a dragon's back. That and the wonder of the true scale of the forests of Elysia when seen spread out below them, expanding off in every direction as far as the eye could see.

At set of the sun Decorum and Blairoggin were formally introduced to their new passengers' counterparts.

Decorum offered only a gruff hello to the moonglider Sirus but Zoozie had already discreetly warned him about his surly nature. Yet it didn't seem to affect the gossamer winged night dweller unduly. Indeed, Alcor, who was Kizzy's moonglider partner to Blairoggin, reacted with similar disdain. These inoffensive little creatures obviously had a much more laid back attitude to dragons, and to life in general. They appeared to have no great fear of 'big' flying either. Perhaps though that had much to do with the fact that moongliders slept soundly during the day and the inbred tenacity with which they clung to a roost when asleep worked just as well whether they were latched onto a tree branch or a dragon's scales. As Bizarh had already found when flying with Mira, it seemed virtually impossible to either dislodge or wake a moonglider during daylight flying, no matter how outrageous his aerial manoeuvres!

And so the now rather expanded group, a trio of trios, sat beneath the almost deserted moonglider roost, illuminated by the soft light of the twin moons that slanted down through the hole in the dark canopy.

"So, what's the plan then?" Decorum broke the awkward silence, still finding it strange to have a cloud-hopper standing on one shoulder and a moonglider clambering over his back as if he were a huge, living climbing frame. The little feet skittering over his scales made him occasionally give an involuntary shiver, a feeling he secretly rather enjoyed.

Blairoggin nodded, unwittingly dislodging the two creatures that had until that moment been perched on his head, causing them to suddenly take to the air and fly briefly around his head before re-alighting. He felt conspicuously like a glorified perch.

Bizarh, with Binnie at his feet and Mira flitting effortlessly through the darkness above him, wondered briefly if they all looked as absurd as they felt.

"Well," the green dragon said. "Niaouli mentioned that we should split up. I reckon we should take the little ones over the brownness, let them pick up the three individual wizard auras and then head off in separate directions to find them."

"Fair play," agreed Decorum.

"Yes." Blairoggin dislodged his passengers for a second time. "One to the hills, one towards the coast and one to the villages. Seems like as good a starting place as any," he added before anyone questioned his apparent attempt to take over as leader. He recalled how Niaouli had said no one should lead.

But no one felt that way. They just saw the wiseness of his words and there was a moment's silence as everyone just looked at everyone else.

"Well, before we go then, I'd just like to wish everyone the best of luck." Bizarh's words were heartfelt.

"And you," said Decorum.

"Yes." Blairoggin remembered just in time not to nod. He suddenly held out a fisted paw. Decorum leant forward and butted his own fist against it. Bizarh wasn't sure of the significance of the gesture, but hesitated only a moment before putting his own fist to theirs. The solemnity of the moment was not lost on the smaller members of the group who also observed the moment of silence before quickly taking up their positions on their chosen dragons' backs.

Blairoggin's voice was quiet but determined.

"Let's go."

One after the other the great beasts flexed their wings, coiled and launched, disappearing into the night sky on the backs of great down draughts of air.

The King was visibly shocked by the news.

His jaw momentarily sagged in a very un-king like way as one of his aides relayed it to him.

"Deserted?" His Royal Highness said incredulously.

"Yes, Sire." The immaculately turned out Elfin servant nodded deeply. "Left their posts, Sire. Absent without leave. Missing from the castle, Sire. Gone, without permission or so much as a word of..."

"Yes!" The King angrily bit off the end of his aide's sentence before managing to bring his anger and shock back under control. "I think you can safely say they have deserted."

The aide nodded once again, but wisely said no more. He waited a moment to see if the King was going to speak again and when he didn't, bowed deeply and withdrew.

"Both Decorum *and* Blairoggin!" The King turned to his Queen, the astonished look still on his face. "I don't understand it at all. Decorum, well, he can be a bit headstrong I know but disloyal? Never. And Blairoggin was, is, one if not the most trusted of my subjects. And the two hardly ever spoke to each other so why both together?"

It was a measure of his fondness for the two missing dragons that he chose not to dwell on the severity of their crime of leaving the castle and its King unguarded. That could be addressed when the time was right and the full facts gathered. After all, was he not known throughout Elysia as a great and just King? He simply wanted to know their reason for desertion before taking any action against them.

The Queen sat opposite her husband in their private chambers, watching the gamut of emotions cross his face.

The chambers themselves were some of the smallest rooms in the entire castle, but still had the very high ceilings and one very large portal window per room that could be found throughout the rest of the building.

She opened her arms in a typically graceful gesture.

"They are both loyal dragons dear, I am sure. They would not have simply left. Not without a very good reason."

Her gentle logic reassured the King, as it always did. It was one of the reasons why he loved her so.

"Of course, you are right. But I must know these reasons. What they have done could be considered treason and I will be expected to act. I don't doubt that the townsfolk are already gossiping about their absence already."

"Undoubtedly." The Queen raised a royal eyebrow. She was, as royalty, considered to be aloof and above the common populous of Talla-Weyre but even so her ears had already picked up snippets of gossip and rumour. The townsfolk were disturbed by this unheard of event.

"But how to find out?" The King lowered his chin onto a clenched fist in the classic thinker's pose. Although not at all stupid, he knew he wasn't the wisest Elf in the Kingdom, after all he had great scholars to do his deep thinking for him, but he liked to give a favourable impression, to those who sought his audience for advice. The pose was one he had originally cultivated a long time ago to help give just such an impression but it had now become a part of his natural character. This unnoticed mannerism made the Queen smile briefly.

From behind His Royal Highness came a polite cough. In response the King didn't look round, but up.

Above him, arching forward was the head of a rather striking dragon of stature. Apparently unperturbed by the current goings on or the obvious confinement of the small room and the ceiling not very far above his head, the beast sat quiet and statue like behind the King, as was his normal post. He even had his own space behind the royal throne in the great hall, free reign of the entire castle and accompanied the King wherever possible.

For Agranth was the King's dragon.

They had both been born at the same moment, although a thousand miles apart, and were destined to be lifelong companions. It had always been this way for when a royal personage was born destined to eventually take a throne, a dragon soul mate always arrived at the same moment. Legend says it is an ancient link between dragons and royal blood, some say it was because of some mysterious magic cast by an ancient wizard long, long ago back in the mists of time. But of course, no one knows for sure, except perhaps the dragons. And they're not telling.

But they must surely know something for even though baby dragons hatched out from their stone eggs far away in the high mountains the females, fiercely protective of their young, knew instantly when a royal blood dragon was born and gave him or her up without qualm. Besides, such dragons were the only ones to emerge with scales and winglets of a metallic colouring.

Agranth, the King's dragon, was magnificent to behold. And big! It was commonly believed that he was very possibly the biggest dragon of stature in the entire kingdom of Elysia. The deep rich gold of his scales along the leading edges of his wings and down the entire length of his broad back emphasised his majestic lines. This flashing colouring lightened down his flanks and across his wing membranes to a lighter, sunshine yellow. Sometimes, when he walked or flew through the sunlight at the right angle, he seemed to shimmer and it was as if for a magical moment all bone and sinew were gone and he were briefly a living, animated splash of liquid gold.

But all this was lost to the King whose current concerns were uppermost in his mind.

"Yes, my friend?" he asked the magnificent beast.

"Might I suggest that I go and look for our absentees?" His deep, mellow voice betrayed no emotion of the news. Whatever thoughts he had about it he kept to himself. "A dragon to find a dragon?"

"But that would leave only the Queen's dragon to oversee the castle."

"I'm sure Cearanth can manage." Agranth permitted himself a half smile.

The Queen nodded in agreement of the gold dragon's appreciation of her own blood dragon's capabilities. Her majesty's dragon Cearanth was the creature in question and the only current female royal blood dragon. The Queen sometimes thought, but never spoke of it, that often the King's dragon was chosen in preference for special tasks or ceremonial duties over her own much loved dragon because she was female. Yet whenever time, event or circumstance had dictated that Cearanth act, had she ever been found wanting in tact, skill or strength? Was she not at this very moment missing from her mistress's side, busy doing a thorough round of the castle in the absence of the two missing castle dragons?

"Yes," the King finally agreed. "I see your wisdom, my friend. Go then and search for them. Bring them back if you can, but at least find out just what has driven or drawn them away. I have questions to answer."

"By your command," said Agranth with a venerable nod.

The King nodded back, then added with a raised eyebrow.

"Is now too soon to start?"

"Not soon enough," muttered Agranth under his breath, itching to fly towards action and adventure. It had been a while. "Your Highnesses."

He bowed quite deeply this time considering the confined space, then moved to the portal window and without another word pushed through and launched himself into space.

The King and Queen moved quickly enough to the window to see the great gold dragon complete an aerial loop above the perimeter castle walls, passing by the window close enough to hear as the Queen called good luck. With that he banked away towards the distant green horizon and started to climb into the blue.

Dusk had come and gone, the evening dark now as night drew inexorably in.

Bizarh had been following the vague directions given by Mira once the moonglider had finally awoken. It appeared that by the time a few days passed after a spell had been cast its aura had already faded quite badly. He imagined it spreading out into the ether like a morning mist to hang in the sky as invisible, thin cloud. After another few days, Mira had also informed him, it would be gone completely. Thus the moonglider could only give somewhat general, 'southish' directions, likewise the other moongliders who had lead Decorum and Blairoggin off in their own directions.

So Bizarh, Mira and Little Binnie had flown south and now found themselves approaching the edge of the wild wood and the hinterland area beyond. A few Elfin villages could be found here, clinging limpet-like to the rim of the deep forest. From his lofty vantage point Bizarh could see the occasional road cutting in their typical straight lines through the less densely timbered transitional landscape. All at once, below and ahead of them at the intersection of several of these lines a big clearing revealed itself. Central in this clearing alongside the most well worn road the green dragon could make out a large thatched building, easily seen because of the lanterns that hung from various brackets around its walls. It was oblong in shape and had the traditional large portal window at one end, but this one going right down to the ground and so doubling as the main door. The biggest and brightest lantern hung above it. Just outside were several beasts of burden and various carts, wagons and rough chariot like transport vehicles.

"I think it a good idea if we stop here and ask if there might be any local wizards about the vicinity." The green dragon came smoothly in over the tree tops before shattering the illusion of gracefulness by thudding down to a jarring halt on the hard packed ground outside the building.

Binnie was instantly apprehensive. She peered over Bizarh's shoulder, unimpressed by the battered condition of the place with its well weathered old brown thatch and slightly sagging timbers. To her the place looked rather squalid.

"What is this place?" she asked.

Bizarh read the large, but faded sign above the big door and knew instantly that there would be people inside from many different walks of life. Surely one within would know of any local wizards. He just grinned into the dark and said boldly.

"That, my friend, is a tavern."

"Is that good?" asked Mira.

In answer Bizarh shrugged, still noticing the unfamiliar feel of the little creatures riding upon his back. He took a deep breath then walked boldly in through the portal door.

The tavern was quite well illuminated by the many lanterns hanging from various points around the walls, suspended above the bar and sitting on the tables that seemed to litter the room. It didn't help the ambience of the place much. This tavern was rough and ready. The bar itself was little more than several long planks laid across upended empty kegs. Behind it were tapped kegs laying on sawn timber trestles. The building was one big room with a high vaulted roof and the bar at one end.

The clientele were also rough and ready. Most were leaning on the bar, which Bizarh briefly thought rather odd considering the number of vacant tables in the place. He did recognise some of the Elfin types before him though. People from some of the villages found along the edge of the forest. They all looked like hard grafters with not a smile to share amongst the lot of them. A few especially surly looking individuals looked as if they might have come from the lakeside area. And was that the faint odour of fish he detected?

All the patrons clutched stained wooden tankards in their fists, each filled to a greater or lesser degree with elvengrog. Several Elves looked much the worse for wear from it too.

As Bizarh walked slowly to the centre of the room a stony silence fell that stopped him in his tracks, aware of every eye upon him.

"That's different," said an unidentified voice. "Don't see too many green dragons round these parts."

"What can I do for you?" grunted the innkeeper from behind the bar. His tone inferred he didn't want the dragon's custom and he looked as if he knew how to work the business end of a shillelagh, was Bizarh's immediate impression.

"Good evening," he announced brightly. "I'm looking for wizards."

Someone laughed out loud and a few others joined in.

"Wizards in general or one wizard in particular," continued the innkeeper as if he hadn't even heard the laughter, no change of expression notable on his hard face.

"Oh, only one." It was Little Binnie, chipping in with an attempt to be helpful, humming into view by lifting off from Bizarh's back and flying over his shoulder to alight carefully down on top of one of the table tops.

"Wassat?" slurred a slightly swaying Elf, staring openly at Binnie.

"A cloud-hopper," answered another, suddenly very alert Elf. "And where there's a cloud-hopper there's usually a..."

Right on cue, a little face peered over Bizarh's shoulder.

"Hello." said Mira in a timid voice. "We're only looking for a wizard with a black line to his spell aura."

The drunken Elf knew nothing of auras or spells but black he understood well enough.

"Thatud be Goth on the lake..."

"Shaddap," said the Elf next to him and cuffed the unfortunate one around the back of the head hard enough to knock off his tattered hat.

Drunk or not, the Elf got the message and pursed his lips together, swayed more emphatically for a moment as if in delayed recoil from the blow, then turned his full attention to the mug of elvengrog in his fist. He slurped it, very loud sounding in the silence that followed the slap but the noise was ignored, all other eyes were locked on to Mira.

The Elves with sense, which was most of them, saw not a moonglider perched on the dragon but a veritable fortune in wing money. Even divided between them all each knew that they could pocket best part of a year's wages if they took advantage of the opportunity before them.

Smoothly transitioning from a surly rabble into a team with a united purpose, some Elves began to sidle around the edges of the walls to get behind the little group and cut off any retreat. Those before the dragon lifted themselves rather too casually away from the bar, setting down their pint pots almost in unison. One of the surly lakeside Elves hissed quietly from the corner of his mouth.

"We'll distract 'im. When yuh get the chance grab the 'glider."

Bizarh's highly sensitive hearing heard every word. He began to back slowly away towards the door, only then aware of the Elves now behind him.

"Now, look..."

"Grab 'im!" came several shouts at once and the Elves rushed the dragon *en masse*.

Bizarh went back onto his haunches, pushing out his front paws in defence, only to find his attention instantly diverted by three burly Elves leaping onto his tail in an attempt to pin it down. Before he could look round to see, someone smashed a chair against his flank. Two enterprising Elves leapt onto the nearest table and vaulted straight onto his back, trying to get directly at Mira. The moonglider immediately lifted off and shot up into the rafters of the tavern, Little Binnie only a wing beat behind.

Bizarh pushed out a wing of his own in time to flick away another Elf who was trying to jump on him, the fellow crashing through more furniture on his unplanned way back to the floor. Elves were swarming all about the dragon now. The three on his tail were hanging grimly on and managing to hold their own in the struggle, the green tail squirming like a snake, but not able to shake them loose. Elves now hung from his neck and two more had produced from somewhere several lengths of rope which were thrown deftly over his shoulders and neck. They were trying to tie him down.

Several of the lakeside Elves had broken off from the main attack and turned their attention towards Mira and Binnie. The thugs drew back and hurled pieces of broken furniture into the roof space to try and bring them down. Bizarh shot out a wing and the lumps of timber impacted the underside of the membrane. Wincing at the pain he tried his best to hold the position but more Elves clambered onto his neck, combining with those pulling on the ropes to drag his head ever nearer the floor. In moments he would be totally immobilised. Now he had no choice.

He began to inhale deeply.

"Look out!" came a shout. "Flamer!"

A quick thinking Elf grabbed a full tankard from the end of the bar and slung the elvengrog straight into Bizarh's open mouth and down his throat.

The green dragon gagged, coughed and spluttered, swallowing a great draught of the potent brew. It was bitter and raw on his throat, sloshing down his gullet and into his stomach, burning all the way. And burned on, seeming to ignite his entire system. The heat roared down to the tip of his tail and thundered up his long neck right into his brain. Bizarh's vision blurred and rippled. He suddenly felt as if his entire body was trying to turn itself inside out.

A strangled cry from one of his attackers wormed into his brain.

"By the Gods! I thought they only existed in stories. He's a Warp dragon! LOOK OUT!!"

All Bizarh was aware of was a great surge of strength surging through him. The Elves however, realising that the tables were suddenly turned, could only look on in shock, surprise and dismay. The scales on the dragon's underbelly retained a green tinge but those covering the rest of his body rippled and went into eclipse, turning almost instantaneously into a rich, glinting bronze. He seemed to somehow swell slightly, as if drawing in a great breath, although this he could not do in his almost helplessly bound condition. His still extended wing visibly expanded both in length and breadth, the other also although unseen, and his talons became dagger like. Two matched pairs of blades flicked suddenly and unexpectedly out from either side of the end of his tail making the Elves close by leap hurriedly back in fright. With a great surge of strength the tail switched and flung away the Elves who were now trying to cling on for dear life. The all completed very ungraceful loops through the air before sprawling, winded, on the floor, while the lethal weapon lashed round, scattering more Elves and smashing what remained of the intact tables. With a thud the blades bit deep into the planking of the bar. The landlord dived hurriedly for cover beneath the elvengrog kegs.

Bizarh exerted his increased strength with a great wrench, lifting up his head, only vaguely noticing the looks of astonishment on the faces of Mira and Binnie. Nor too did he take much notice of the Elves, some still clinging to short lengths of their snapped rope, who were flung from the bronze neck. Two unwillingly joined the landlord in a tangle of arms and legs beneath the kegs. One Elf actually went up and out through the thatching of the roof. Where he landed, or in what condition no one could tell, or even cared at that moment. Every Elf who could still stand or crawl was doing his damnedest to get out of the building, falling over each other in the rush for the exits.

Now free, Bizarh finally managed to draw in that much desired deep breath. Tilting his head back and opening his jaws wide in a silent wolf howl, the air whistled audibly as it was drawn in. Everyone knew what happened next. Those still inside the tavern threw themselves to the floor, out of the nearest window or under any cover they could find. Mira and Binnie flew like arrows into the furthest corner of the roof.

Then Bizarh let go, to the accompaniment of a great roar from deep in his throat.

An astounding thing happened. The great tongue of flame that lashed out from his jaws was green! It still had heat enough to be felt by those nearby and dazzled the eye like sunlight through an emerald lens, but somehow it didn't burn. The fire licked over the roof beams and thrust into the thatch yet didn't ignite it.

Bizarh, even in his wide-eyed and uncontrolled state, didn't seem at all satisfied with the result of his flare. Still both determined and desperate to get out of the tavern and away from his attackers he flexed his larger, bronze wings and, without regard for any obstacles or persons around him, coiled and launched. Straight up and out through the roof! Shredded thatch flew in all directions, broken roof timbers crashed down around the still cowering Elves, while the tavern walls sagged sickeningly outwards, but somehow still held together. And the dragon was gone.

For a long moment after the last of the debris hit the floor there was a deafening silence. Then the quiet hum of fast beating wings swirled the dusty air in the roof space as Mira and Little Binnie flew out of the gaping roof hole and into the night in pursuit of their surprising friend.

An odd thing. As the pair flew away Binnie took a last look back over her shoulder. The tavern was now no more than a great heap of wreckage with Elves staggering aimlessly around outside it. But at either ends of the gaping roof the remaining thatch, once old, brown and dead, was now a rich green, with each and every stem carrying a full ear of wheat at the end.

The elder protects the younger. As it has always been.

4
Pressing Ahead

Blairoggin, Kizzy and Alcor were heading out over the wildwoods back towards the inhabited hinterland. Alcor had guided the Keeper of the Keys throughout the night while Kizzy slept on the dragon's broad back.

The castle dragon did his best, and his best was very good, to keep his flight stable and even, not wishing to jog or jar the small creatures he carried. As usual he didn't say much and the moonglider didn't seem to mind. But that didn't stop the pair communicating. A quiet suggestion of going slightly right and the dragon silently obliged. A tad left and a gentle, angled sweep achieved the desired course correction with a minimum of fuss.

As the night drew towards its close Blairoggin decided that a rest period was in order. It was best to pace oneself if it wasn't known how far the journey was going to be. He went into a gently inclined dive and dropped down to just above the tree tops, flying as slowly as he could until finding an open glade. Dipping even lower towards the ground and angling his wings just the right amount to scrub off what speed was left he swept quietly in, executed the perfect stall and dropped gently to the soft earth landing on all four paws. Kizzy didn't even stir.

"We'll rest here a while," he said quietly to Alcor who had already lifted off and was now flitting effortlessly back and forth in front of the dragon's huge head. Blairoggin had no difficulty seeing the moonglider in the darkness. "But we'll be on the move again before you next awake. Which way then, my little friend?"

Alcor dropped his head coyly at the complimentary acknowledgement.

"Keep going towards the point where the sun first shows itself above the horizon. But stop before you reach the very edge of the woodlands. Beyond there I know no landmarks."

Blairoggin nodded. "Yes, best to check with the guide before going too far."

"You are a very wise dragon," said Alcor respectfully.

"Why, thank you." Blairoggin closed his eyes. Alcor wasn't sure, but thought for a moment that if the great beast before him had been covered in skin instead of dark scales, he might have actually seen him blushing.

A thin line of red began to make itself seen along the far horizon.

"Here comes the false dawn," said the moonglider. "I'll be going to sleep now. Look after Kizzy for me."

"I'll take good care of you both." There was an undeniable certainty in the dragon's voice. "Now, up you go."

"Thank you." And with that the moonglider flew up over the horned head and landed lightly on the scaly back. "G'night, great one," he said softy and snuggled as best he could against his genial host.

Blairoggin just fanged a warm but unseen smile into the half light and lay down himself and settled into a very loose coil, careful of course not to disturb either of his little passengers.

When he awoke he found the sun high in the sky and Kizzy the cloud-hopper waiting patiently on the ground directly in front of him. Sleepily lifting his head the dragon flexed his wings in an impressive stretch then offered up a truly gaping, fang filled monster of a yawn. When he at last closed his jaws Kizzy was nowhere to be seen.

"Er... hello?"

Rustling from a large clump of bushes a good distance off gave away the cloud-hopper's position and the dragon allowed himself another rare smile.

"Come on out," he said softly. "I'm very sorry. I didn't mean to frighten you."

The little one emerged timidly from her cover and gingerly approached.

"I... I wasn't that frightened," she stammered. "Just... just a bit startled is all."

"Of course." He brought his head back down to ground level. "So other than a little startled, how are we today? Did you enjoy your sleep?"

"Yes thank you, but not I think as much as you enjoyed yours."

Blairoggin just cocked one scaly eye ridge in question.

"You were snoring so loudly I thought every forest creature in Elysia must have heard you," she explained.

"Do I really snore?" he asked, a disbelieving tone in his voice.

Kizzy nodded emphatically.

Blairoggin considered this new fact for a few moments before dismissing it with a shrug. True or not, there wasn't much he could do about it. He did not make the connection that his fearsome reputation around the castle of Talla-Weyre was due at least in part to the monstrous, nerve jangling roars and snorts that occasionally came booming resonantly up from deep in the dark bowels of the castle where he was known to prowl.

A silence fell between the huge castle dragon and the tiny forest dweller.

Kizzy began to feel intimidated again and so, to prove at least to herself if to no one else, that she could rise above such fear she hummed up into the air. Blairoggin watched with one crystalline eye as the cloud-hopper flew up alongside his head then perched on his crown, squarely between his stubby horns. Craning her neck forward to come down into the dragon's view she asked.

"How far have we come and is there much further to go?"

Blairoggin had to go cross-eyed to bring the now upside down face of Kizzy into focus. He was always such a serious and stern dragon. So how come these harmless little creatures found it so easy to make him act and look like a chump?

"We are nearing the edge of the deep forest. Alcor says not to fly on too far without his guidance so I guess we must be getting close. So we'll wait a while longer I think."

"Thank you." Kizzy nodded an upside down nod then drew back out of sight, settling down between the horns.

"Huh, you're welcome." Blairoggin felt somehow dismissed but held his head steady so as not to dislodge the cloud-hopper, uncrossed his now straining eyes and waited patiently for the exploding little green swirls in his vision to subside.

After flying in a straight line for several hours the range of mountains ahead of them still seemed to be as far away as ever. It was these mountains that Sirus the moonglider had indicated they should head towards, before he settled down on the dragon's back for his daytime sleep.

Decorum, more used to the jumble of buildings and short travelling distances in and around Talla-Weyre was still having a little trouble coming to terms with the great expanses he now found himself in. While he was in the company of Blairoggin and Bizarh the greenness and space seemed of little consequence. But now, out on his own over unfamiliar territory he suddenly realised he was, if not intimidated, at least rather daunted by it all.

"It's all a bit bland," he said gruffly. "All this open greenness mile after mile after mile. How do you put up with it?"

To Zoozie it appeared that even the great dragon's normal conversation was harsh, with an aggressive tone and she suddenly felt quite intimidated at this sudden and unexpected attempt at conversation. They weren't flying at a great speed and the rush of air past them did not smother the words so she couldn't feign deafness and politely ignore him. His question demanded an answer. The cloud-hopper looked out over the forest canopy spread out beneath them. It was true, she realised, that from this height it did all appear very much alike.

"Well... I must admit I've never given it much thought, but I've also never seen it from this high up before."

"Huh!" grunted the Gate Keeper. "Now, Talla-Weyre. There's a view for you. And full of life too."

"Is it green?" asked Zoozie. At that Decorum almost stalled his flight in surprise. It was the last question he expected to be asked about the bustling capital of Elysia. The city was a lot of things but could never be said to be green.

"Do you mean to say you've never been there?"

"Don't even know where it is," replied the cloud-hopper, keeping to herself the addition of 'and I don't really want to know either'.

"You don't know what you're missing, my little friend." Decorum's voice took on a softer tone and he cocked his head slightly to one side as he considered his home town. At no time during this did his flight line deviate as much as a single degree. Then he stared off into the distance, taking a moment's consideration before speaking again.

"It's really something. The jumble of houses, inns, markets and shops all spilling out around the foot of the castle and the entire thing wrapped protectively up in the city wall. The whole place is filled with bustle and life as the people who live there go about their business. And slap bang in the middle of it all, overseeing the entire place, is the castle of the King and Queen. D'you know, from high in the air the city looks like one great eye with the castle as the pupil. If Elysia were a great, living being, Talla-Weyre would be the eye and behind it lies the brain that makes the whole thing work. I suppose really that Talla-Weyre and their royal majesties are the life force of Elysia."

Zoozie just sat, open mouthed in astonishment at the sudden grandeur, and rich eloquence of the unexpected speech. Decorum too was a little surprised. He never realised he'd had it in him. Perhaps his exposure to the great lands and forests of Elysia had awakened his love for the place. Maybe coming out to the wildwoods was proving beneficial after all.

"Well... er, yes." The gruffness dropped quickly back into place. "Anyway, It's something to see all right."

"And you have an important job there?" Zoozie was now much more curious about her huge partner.

"Oh yes. I am the Gate Keeper," Decorum pronounced proudly.

"The gate. Do they only have one gate in their fence then?"

Only a few days earlier Decorum would have flown into an instant rage at the blatant insult to his city and his own position within it, but he knew that little Zoozie spoke in complete innocence. How would she know otherwise if she had never been there?

To the cloud-hopper's surprise the blue dragon let out a great laugh.

"Fence, that's a good one. No, no, my little friend, no fences, and actually only four entrances to the city itself. One at each of the four points of the compass. But there is only one gate into the castle itself. Through that must go all who would wish to see the King and it is the job and duty of the keeper of that gate to keep out all the undesirables and greet all the dignitaries."

"An important job then," said Zoozie.

"Oh yes." Decorum's chest puffed out with pride. "And I am that Gate Keeper."

It was quite a magnanimous statement and the cloud-hopper was rather at a loss as to quite what to say next.

"Well... Then I can honestly say that it is a great honour to be travelling with such a distinguished and important dragon." She hoped it was the right reply.

Decorum nodded his head at the compliment, Zoozie nodded hers at the success of her sudden diplomacy and the pair lapsed into a now much more genial and comfortable silence as they travelled onwards over the greenness of the forest towards the distant mountains.

Little Binnie and Mira finally found Bizarh standing quietly in a forest glade a few miles away from the site of the wrecked tavern. The false dawn was just beginning to show far off on the distant horizon and when their search had originally proved fruitless Binnie had feared she might have to bed down her moonglider companion and continue to search alone.

But there he now stood, a confused look on his face, as the little forest dwellers descended out of the darkness above the tree tops and settled lightly on the ground before him. He appeared to be his normal self now, all green scales and with his amiable disposition restored.

"Hello," he said rather lamely as the pair came to rest.

They didn't reply at first but scrutinised the forest dragon carefully to ensure there were no bulging muscles, tail blades or sharp, hooked talons.

"Is it all right to go on up?" asked Mira rather unexpectedly. He was well aware of the fast approaching daylight and needed to sleep, but wanted first to be sure if his now customary perch was still available and not hazardous.

Bizarh just cocked an eyebrow at the unexpected question.

"Why wouldn't it be?"

"Yes, I should think so," Binnie said quietly to her friend, then looked up at Bizarh. "Well you have to admit, that was a pretty impressive and quite terrifying display you put on in the tavern."

"It was?"

"Don't you remember?" asked Binnie, astounded.

"Only vaguely." Bizarh dipped his head so he could scratch it with one of his claws. Mira took advantage of this action to fly up over the horned head and onto the dragon's back.

"Well if it's all right with you I'll get some sleep. You know which way to go." And with that he latched securely onto the green scales, spread his small but magnificent wings wide and was instantly asleep as the first rays of the sun broke through to slant steeply across onto him.

All the while Binnie continued to stare at Bizarh.

"You've no clear recollection of what you just did?"

"Well, sort of. I remember entering the bar and then being attacked. After that it all gets a bit fuzzy. I do remember a tremendous roaring inside me and a sudden feeling of great power. Then all I recall is a burning need to get out of there. After that everything seemed to let go all at once."

"And you're not hurt?" Binnie flicked her head from side to side as she quickly checked what she could of him in the early light. "No bones broken, bruises or cuts?"

Bizarh shrugged. "It doesn't seem so."

"Well, that's quite amazing," breathed Binnie. "I saw you knock men flying, smash furniture to splinters then break stout ropes like they were spiders webs before flying straight up through a thatched ceiling without even slowing down for roof beams, cross timbers or anything!"

"Really?" There was genuine awe in Bizarh's voice and he flexed his wings and inspected their leading edges. "Not a mark. Are you sure?"

"Oh, yes."

The pair lapsed into a silence and let their thoughts run their course. Bizarh tried hard but could only really remember the purely instinctive actions he had taken after his body had erupted. Everything else was shrouded in a mental mist.

Little Binnie decided to keep her own council. But she had seen. She knew it was the elvengrog that had set off the remarkable change in her green friend, but that power to change must have already been within him to start with. Was still within him. She looked up into the crystalline eyes as the early light revealed more.

"One of the Elves shouted something as you changed," she said slowly. "Do you know anything of what he said. These, 'warp' dragons?"

"Nope," was the flat answer.

"Me neither." She shook her head. "But the Elves obviously thought you are one."

"Is that good or bad?"

"I don't know." She shrugged. "But you seem all right now. How do you feel?"

Bizarh closed his eyes.

"I feel... actually, I feel rather good." Bizarh flexed and stretched his great frame. He certainly looked what he was. A fit, healthy young dragon of stature, in prime condition. "Ready for anything."

"Well, I don't know about you," said the cloud-hopper. "But after all that excitement I'm just about ready for a rest. Do you think we could stay here for a few hours before we set off again?"

"I don't see why not." Bizarh nodded, although he wasn't in the least bit sleepy. In contrast he felt invigorated. He couldn't remember when he'd ever felt better. "Get some sleep. I'll scout the area ahead then collect you before we carry on."

"Ahead which way?"

"Why, towards the Lakeland of course. Didn't you hear that Elf mention a wizard there called, what was it now, Goth?"

Well you remember that all right, thought Binnie, but she never said, just nodded.

"I suppose that's what Mira meant when he said 'you know which way to go'."

"Exactly."

And with that the remarkable green forest dragon winked at his companion, coiled and launched effortlessly into the early morning blue.

* * * * *

The day so far had gone well and the Keeper of the Keys and his two companions had made good time. Visible now on the horizon, but still a way off, was the different colouring where the wild woods gave way to the inhabited, farmed lands.

It was late afternoon and during his pre-flight directions that morning Alcor had said he'd seen the aura more clearly. They appeared to be getting closer to their objective.

The same thoughts were running through Kizzy's head and the little cloud-hopper was wondering just how far Blairoggin would go on before stopping to get more directions. She trusted in his judgement. Besides, in a few more hours it would once again be dark and then Alcor could guide on in person. It really was a bit of a nuisance that the moonglider couldn't stay awake during the daylight hours. Still, then he wouldn't be a moonglider would he.

Just as this less than profound thought rose to the surface of the cloud-hopper's mind the little patch of Elysia she occupied went suddenly dark. As if the sun above had been instantly eclipsed. Startled to find Blairoggin's broad back unexplainably in shadow she turned up towards the sun, only to find the hot orb obscured from her vision by the dark silhouette of a rapidly descending dragon. A big one and rapidly descending onto them!

"Blairoggin!" she screeched and the dark blue dragon beneath her turned his head, saw at the last moment the fast approaching dragon on its attack run out of the sun and banked sharply to one side. He didn't really think his unknown aerial assailant actually intended to collide with him in mid-air, but was trying to startle and confuse him. He was succeeding!

The huge, diving dragon went by with mere inches to spare and executed a magnificently controlled high G turn that used his greater speed to loop him back up over the re-stabilising dark blue dragon and once again regain his higher altitude advantage.

In reply Blairoggin himself tried for more height but was hampered by both his concern for his small passengers and the rather good harassing tactics of the bigger dragon.

After several fruitless swoop, dive and loop manoeuvres Blairoggin knew he was being comprehensively outflown. Even though he was still several thousand feet above the rolling green canopy he knew there was no way he would be able to reach the edge of the forest unless he could get by the big dragon. And he couldn't see that happening right now.

Avoiding the diving beast one more time and again losing more altitude in the manoeuvre, he accepted defeat and levelled out and slowed his speed in surrender.

"Who is it?" asked Kizzy, breathless from hanging tightly on during the frightening aerial manoeuvres. She still didn't know that both dragons were showing some restraint in their flying skills. Blairoggin in deference to his passengers and the big dragon so that his harassment was enough to display his superiority and get the others undivided attention.

"That," said Blairoggin in blunt admiration, "is Agranth, the King's dragon."

"He frightens me."

"He frightens most people."

"But what does he want?"

"Let's find out."

Blairoggin continued his flat, steady glide and waited.

Sure enough, once the King's dragon was satisfied about the dark blue dragon's capitulation he came down over him and matched his flight, all the time keeping the height advantage.

"What do you want, Agranth?" said Blairoggin loudly.

"You are to return to Talla-Weyre now," came back the booming, authoritative voice.

"But I have very important work to..."

"I don't care what you want," interrupted the King's dragon. "You will return to Talla-Weyre with me, now! There you can explain the desertion of your duties to the King himself."

Even Kizzy could detect the hint of both menace and enjoyment in the voice of the huge, gold coloured dragon.

"Look, you don't understand..." Blairoggin pleaded, which Kizzy found quite disturbing. Her big friend was always so bold, decisive and confident. It just wasn't right to hear him cower like this.

"Now!" shouted Agranth, quickly annoyed that he should have to repeat himself more than once and have his orders questioned. He was the King's dragon. To emphasise his displeasure he deftly banked and hooked up the tip of Blairoggin's wing with his own. Unprepared, the Keeper of the Keys immediately lost his trim, destabilised and spiralled earthward before regaining control to swoop back onto an even keel.

Kizzy, also unprepared, only just managed to keep her purchase. She didn't have enough breath left to scream, but the terror in her gasps was plain enough.

"Right!" said Blairoggin determinedly to himself. He eyed the once more approaching Agranth with a steely eye then went into a steep dive down towards the green canopy below.

Agranth, the disbelief on his face quickly turning to anger at this latest display of disobedience, was after the dark blue dragon in an instant.

Watching the gold dragon's high speed approach Kizzy finally found her voice, but the only sound that came out was a loud screech of fear. Loud enough to make Alcor, who until that moment had somehow still remained asleep, jerk awake. Not knowing what was going on, he barely had enough time to look around him, squinting at the daylight's brightness before Blairoggin executed a tight left turn and only just avoided Agranth's dive.

"Hang on!" he shouted and briefly inverted as he looped the loop in an attempt to get above Agranth.

But the gold dragon was powerful, smooth and very skilful. He stood on one wingtip, pulled an incredibly tight turn and went just a few feet past Blairoggin's nose, making him shy away, once more losing speed. Again, by superior flying skills, Agranth kept his height advantage and Blairoggin found himself even lower.

And that's how it was for the next few minutes. Blairoggin trying to out manoeuvre the bigger dragon to no avail, his little passengers hanging on in wide-eyed fear while the great gold dragon forced them down. It was inevitable. Agranth was the King's dragon, flew all the time and could practise whenever he wanted. In contrast Blairoggin normally only flew at night and also had passengers to consider. There was no flying manoeuvre Blairoggin could do that Agranth could not do faster and more efficiently. In a short time Blairoggin found himself flying only a few dozen feet above the leafy green expanse, out of airspace and out of options. He desperately scanned the treetops while Kizzy and Alcor cowered in the shadow of the dragon above them.

"What now?" Kizzy cried. "We can't go with him. What about the spreading brownness, the wizards and what Crystal said would happen if we don't do anything about it?"

"I know!" barked Blairoggin sharply, frustrated at being unable to extract himself from his situation.

"I saw it," said Alcor suddenly.

"Saw what?" asked Kizzy, suddenly surprised.

"Not now," cut in Blairoggin. "We've other problems to deal with at this moment."

"Well?" shouted Agranth. "I will toy with you no longer. There is nowhere to land. You cannot out fly me. Admit defeat and return with me. Now. I will tell the King you flew bravely."

Blairoggin just scoffed. Nowhere to land, he thought. Of course! That's it! He craned his neck and brought his head in close to his little friends.

"Hang on tight," he whispered. "I'm going to do a Bizarh."

And with that he flew right down until his feet were almost skimming the tree tops. Agranth followed him down and allowed himself a small laugh of congratulation. His quarry had now sandwiched himself between the impenetrable forest canopy and his victor.

Then, to his immense surprise, the dark blue dragon disappeared.

Blairoggin had decelerated until he was flying as slowly as possible, then executed a sharp stall and virtually crashed, in what Bizarh would call a normal landing, through the tree tops to thump to the forest floor in a shower of broken branches. Swiftly he backed into the semi-darkness, away from the circle of light that now illuminated a small section of the ground, the sunshine lancing in through the hole in the canopy he had just made. If his plan worked, Agranth would turn and come back to try and see down into the hole. Now everything came down to timing.

He drew in a deep breath.

Both Kizzy and Alcor knew what happened next. They flew off the scaly back and retreated hurriedly into the trees.

Blairoggin exhaled. To his little companions' utter surprise nothing happened. The pocket of bright air in the sunlit clearing hazed and shimmered, but that was it. Then the shimmering air began to rise up to the mouth of the hole in the canopy. At that moment the light dimmed as Agranth, flying as slowly as he could, appeared over the hole having turned above the greenery and returned to stare in curiosity at the gap where his prey had disappeared.

Blairoggin cried "help!" and the gold dragon banked on one wingtip and came right down over the hole. And then Blairoggin spat out a single bright spark.

At the same moment Agranth smelled the volatile gaseous mixture it ignited. A bright ball of fire erupted upwards out of the tree tops and briefly engulfed him. Of course, he was not even really singed. A fire breathing dragon that was not himself fire proof would be very silly. But what did happen was on top of being completely surprised, the fireball robbed the dragon of the air that supported him in his slow speed flight. His lift was instantly gone and before he could react he plummeted down through the hole and crashed in a heap on the forest floor.

Blairoggin was on him in a flash, pinning his wings with his paws and entwining his own tail around Agranth's to ensure he could neither regain his feet or take to the air.

There was a long moment, locked tightly together as they were, before either of them spoke.

Agranth had never been beaten before. Physically, it would take more than a few flames and a fall to hurt him, but his pride had taken a severe battering. But still he could not deny the admiration he felt for the dragon that had outwitted him and Agranth was not one to bear any ill will against a worthy opponent. He admitted defeat and relaxed his powerful frame.

Blairoggin kept a tight grip on the gold dragon until he felt that moment come. Only then did he allow himself some self congratulation. Bizarh's strange manoeuvre had won the contest for him. He'd tell the forest dragon about it some day. But he did not relinquish his hold on Agranth quite yet.

"Now, my friend," he said quietly. "Will you allow me to explain why I left my post and why it would not be wise to return to Talla-Weyre with you? Or do I have to tie you up to keep your attention?"

The King's dragon even managed somehow to be quite gracious in defeat. His deep, mellow voice showed no hint of malice.

"That will not be necessary. If you would just kindly remove yourself from me, Blairoggin, and if I may say, a fine contest."

"Contest?!" gasped Kizzy and the pair hummed down from their high perch.

"And please, introduce me to your two little friends."

Blairoggin couldn't help but be impressed by Agranth's fine manner and regal tone even in defeat and without a word he slid off the dragon and backed up to a nearby tree, watching as his big opponent lifted to his feet, effortlessly shook every scrap of forest debris from his scales then settled rather neatly into a loose coil opposite him.

Kizzy and Alcor, also watching in silence as they hovered in the air turned to Blairoggin, flew up to his head and perched on top of it between his short horns. The Keeper of the Keys once again felt he made a rather foolish figure, especially in front of the King's dragon who, only moments before had been blasted from the sky yet still somehow managed to look rather splendid.

But Agranth did not appear to see Blairoggin as the dark blue dragon saw himself, even if he might think it. His expression showed neither mirth nor concern.

"This... this is Kizzy and the moonglider is Alcor." Blairoggin brought his head forward by way of introduction. The little forest dwellers bowed as best they could from their perch. To their surprise Agranth nodded deeply in return.

"Pleased to meet you both," he said politely. The pair didn't speak, just happy that Blairoggin immediately drew his head back up again and gave them a little space. To say they were intimidated would be an understatement. They weren't sure if it was more unnerving to be buzzed by the King's dragon, or to be charmed by him.

"Now, Blairoggin," said the dangerously charming one. "Oh, Keeper of the Keys and deserter of his post. What have you got to say for yourself?"

The last part made Blairoggin visibly wince and to her surprise Kizzy felt for her big, uncomfortable friend.

"I have much to tell you," started Blairoggin. "And when I am done I hope you will look more favourably on me and understand why I, and Decorum, have left the warmth and security of Talla-Weyre and come far out into the wild woods of Elysia."

Agranth simply folded his forepaws across his broad chest and sat back to listen.

Blairoggin took a deep breath and tried to explain as fully as he could how he and Decorum had received a mysterious telepathic call about a strange green forest dragon, the meeting at Unicorn Glade and the little friends who now accompanied him. But most of all he spoke about the creeping brownness.

Until that part Agranth had listened without expression. It would have been much easier for Blairoggin if his audience of one had at least gasped or scoffed at some point, but the totally expressionless look from the King's dragon was quite unsettling. But at the mention of the brownness he slowly raised one eye ridge, sensing this as the source of the rather unbelievable tall tale, and said slowly.

"Tell me more of this."

Glad of the prompt Blairoggin obliged, explaining how Niaouli had somehow known of the three spells and their unfortunate clashing together to create a curse upon the earth that threatened to destroy everything.

Agranth tried not to show it as his curiosity changed to concern at this point. Blairoggin, Kizzy and Alcor thought that he now feared for the survival of his King's domain. In fact his thinking was on a different line. For at this moment he still doubted the full truthfulness of the tale, but immediately realised that if what was being relayed was even a half truth, a steadfast, unshakeable royally proclaimed law of Elysia had been broken by someone. His long experience of dealing with and being around those who came into the presence of the King, other members of royalty, noblemen, scholars and wizards alike, gave him a sound overall knowledge of the laws of the land. Laws governing everything from the normal day-to-day running of the kingdom of Elysia right through to those relating to court and royal obligations. This included the dispensing of summary justice and special regulations governing wizards and some of their magical activities. And he knew without doubt that for even plant life to be totally extinguished by magic, as told to him by those with him now, then a wizard somewhere within the realm had set forth a death spell. The one spell hardly ever used and NEVER without the express permission of the King himself. And Agranth, always at the King's side, knew for a fact that special permission had not been given in a long time.

"How long ago do you think this brownness started?" he asked almost too casually.

"Not more than a week or so ago," chipped in Kizzy.

"Hmmm." Agranth cupped his lower jaw in one huge paw. "And it's the result of wizard magic, you're sure?"

Alcor, who up till that moment was having great difficulty in keeping his eyes open, jerked awake.

"Oh yes. I saw it."

"It's true." Blairoggin backed up his little friends. "Moongliders can see the auras of wizards who cast spells, you know."

"Really?" There was genuine surprise in Agranth's tone. "I thought it was only the wizards themselves who could do that."

"I saw it," said Alcor for the third time.

"Yes, at the brownness. We know." Kizzy tried to shush her partner from repeating himself further.

"No no. I saw it just now. While we were whizzing around in the sky."

Blairoggin tried to look up at the creature on his brow, going cross-eyed in the process.

"Are you sure? The wizard we've been tracking. You saw his aura just now?"

"Yes!" said Alcor emphatically.

"Do you think you can keep awake long enough to show us exactly where?"

Alcor was so tired, but he nodded.

Blairoggin turned to face Agranth.

"If you would accompany me and my friends until we find this wizard, I hope we can soon show you some proof of what I say. If you are not then convinced I will go freely back with you to Talla-Weyre and throw myself upon the mercy of the King."

Agranth raised another eye ridge and pretended to consider the offer. He would of course agree to the terms, if for no other reason than to keep this adventure going. He was rather enjoying the whole thing, defeat and all. But he was a dragon of royal connection and so had to act accordingly and he felt it his duty to follow up on any claim, no matter how wild, that an inflexible law of Elysia had been broken. After a few silent moments he nodded courteously and eyed the little moonglider.

"Lead on little one, and I will follow. For now."

The mellow voice with just a hint of menace shocked Alcor back to full wakefulness. He cowered against one of Blairoggin's horns.

"Let... let's go then," he said shakily and flew straight down on to Blairoggin's back, glad to be momentarily out of the gold dragon's sight. Kizzy joined him and both dragons rose to their feet.

"After you then." Agranth offered the lead, knowing full well that they knew he could not be escaped. Blairoggin just nodded in reply, coiled and launched up through the hole in the tree tops, Agranth only a few wing beats behind him.

TRAVELLER BEWARE!
PHOEBE MOON
1997

5

A Wizard Collection

Decorum eyed the towering mountains directly ahead of him, black in silhouette against the soft pale glow of the sky beyond. Unusually, both moons were full together and they cast enough light for it to seem almost as if the dragon flew through a very overcast day. He looked earthward and amended his thought: like a dull day apart from the impenetrable blackness of the shadows.

Even as he watched the ground below the last of the thick wildwoods rapidly thinned and in the time it took for the Gate Keeper to look briefly up at the mountains to check his bearings and return to his downward gaze the trees had all but gone. Replaced by raggedy patchworks of fields, ditches and straggly hedgerows. The occasional glint of a lantern lit window from an isolated cottage or farmstead provided intermittent pinpoints of brightness against the softly moonwashed, yet deeply shadowed, arable lands.

The dragon's meandering attention was immediately restored to clarity as he became aware of one of his diminutive passengers crawling along his neck against the steady push of the slipstream. Sirus struggled on up, reaching the twin horns on the dragon's head before perching himself securely between them. For long moments he stared silently into the apparently empty night sky ahead of them before speaking.

"We are drawing near, O great one," he said loudly in an attempt to make himself heard above the soft rush of air that swept past.

Decorum heard well enough, but if he was impressed or honoured by the moonglider's accolade it didn't show in his voice.

"How far?"

"Not too much farther I think." Sirus looked down at the ground that rushed past so far below. A smile crossed his face, he never could get over the thrill of flying at such speed and altitude even though the great beast he rode considered both things to be relatively low. He briefly wondered just how fast a dragon of stature could fly, and whether he would be able to hang on. Decorum just grunted, which Sirus took to mean that he should impart a bit more information. Not wishing to anger his companion he quickly added. "I think the wizard we seek is nearby in the high foothills of those mountains ahead."

Decorum nodded, only just in time remembering to control his head enough so as not to unseat his companion.

"Will we reach there before dawn?"

"Ah... I think so." Sirus wasn't really sure, surprised to be consulted on such a thing as dragon speed. He could only guess at their actual velocity.

"Good," came the deep voice from directly beneath Sirus. "Then I reckon it best if I settled down somewhere before the dawn and put you up as it were for the coming day. Zoozie can watch over you once she wakes while I go and get the wizard and... er..." There was a long silence before Decorum said quietly, "What then?"

Sirus also fell into a silence, unsure if Decorum was just talking to himself or actually asking the little moonglider what to do. Rather than be rude and ignore the question, he struggled to find an appropriate reply.

"Well... I really don't know." He pondered for a moment more before adding softly, "I wish Niaouli was here, she'd know what to do."

"That's it!" said Decorum to Sirus's complete astonishment. "Exactly the same thought as I had," he bluffed. "We'll all go straight back to Unicorn Glade." He again almost nodded in self agreement to the sudden and very simple plan.

"Er... right." What else could Sirus do but agree?

"Settled then," said Decorum, his voice immediately more gruffly confident now they had an agreed plan of action. "OK, let's crack on." And with that he raised his head slightly to help Sirus return to his normal position upon his back. Once satisfied his little friend was secure the Gate Keeper upped the tempo of his wing beats and accelerated through the semi-darkness towards the Elysian mountains, eyes now beginning to search ahead for a suitable landing place.

Bizarh too had finally reached the edge of the great forest and also held his course to fly steadily on, out over the marsh lands that separated the greenwoods from the watery expanse that was the Great Lake. But he couldn't see across its waters yet. It was still a short way ahead, but he would not have been able to see the lake in any case for even before the arrival of the imminent dawn it was possible to see the first tendrils of swirling mist that reached some distance inland across the marshes. Tendrils that all led back to a great cloak of mist that hung dank and heavy above the waters of the lake, the mist present to a greater or lesser degree for most of the time.

As he drew closer the scene below him went through a rapid change. The countryside's colour seemed to wilt away, becoming more and more dull and sallow looking until, as the flyers crossed the lake shore the mist that covered the waters had reduced all the surrounding area to a sullen grey. Thinner over solid ground the fog allowed a hazy view of the village that hunkered by the lakeside where watery lantern lights fought in vain against the smothering damp. On the lake itself the mist was thick and denied any view of the still, deep waters. The almost solid looking greyness there swam and eddied in lethargic swirls as the breathless breeze stirred it into sluggish motion. It didn't look natural, almost alive somehow and a shudder rippled down Bizarh's spine. He averted his gaze and concentrated on the humping ridge of an island that emerged from the mist some way ahead. Dark in contrast to the blanket of surrounding grey it took the dragon a few moments to realise that it was visible only because of the approaching dawn. It seemed that even the sun was reluctant to show itself over this awful place and yet in the half light he could already see the castle that stood at the summit of this disembodied mound of land.

Bizarh, as he approached with the receding night at his back, witnessed the rising of the sun on the horizon directly in front of him. As it appeared above the mist it thrust the castle into deep silhouette and threw its long shadow towards him like dark, spiny fingers reaching out for him across the surface of the swirling grey. A grey that greedily absorbed the early sunlight and only changed one feeble shade lighter in colour as if in defiance of the bright orb.

"It... it's here." The quietness of Mira's voice did nothing to hide the moonglider's fear. "I can see the aura quite clearly now and such... such blackness. I'm frightened."

"Don't worry little one," said Bizarh with as much confidence as he could muster. He didn't feel all that confident himself. "We'll be all right. I'll look after you."

"Yes," echoed little Binnie rather too boldly. "Nothing will happen while we're with Bizarh. Why don't you get on to sleep?"

"I can't," came back the timid voice. "I'm too scared."

"Well, like I said, don't worry." Bizarh nodded towards the castle they were approaching. "We'll go straight in, tell the wizard what's happening back in the forest and I'm sure as soon as he understands he'll be sure to want to help." It was a reasonable enough statement, but it didn't help him to keep a grip on his confident tone. "We'll be out of this sorry looking place in no time at all."

With that he slightly adjusted his wing membranes, shifted his centre of gravity and went into a shallow dive, beginning his approach to the dark castle. Like his little passengers, he too for some reason found himself holding his breath.

As they reached the great pile of stonework it developed into something of an anticlimax. When the details of the fortress became clearer it looked less intimidating. The walls had very few windows, the perimeter wall turrets were topped by dumpy, hard looking castellations and the outer barrier surrounded a single large building within. This building filled most of the inner enclosure and from its centre a single tower thrust up into the air, twice as high as all the other structures around it.

The castle overall was quite large, but the courtyard was in comparison very small and Bizarh circled the place slowly in search of somewhere to set down. He got no help from below, the place seemed to be completely deserted.

"What now?" asked Binnie.

"Dunno... s'pose we'd best land outside and try to find a door somewhere."

At that moment a light flared suddenly out high up on the central tower, bringing their attention to a previously unnoticed portal there. The lantern drew Bizarh in like a moth and as he slowly approached it became clear that the portal was a regular dragon door. At its base a wide stone ledge jutted out, a plinth offering the perfect landing point for a flyer, far above the ground and sprawling building work below.

"What do you think...?" Binnie was unsure.

"He's obviously had that built with dragons in mind. Probably had several visits before. Perhaps he has dragons in regularly or even commands one of his own?" Bizarh wasn't sure either, but gave a resigned shrug. "There's nowhere else to land and we do need to see this wizard, right?" Not waiting for an answer he did one more circuit of the castle, came in as slowly as he could and rather skilfully managed to execute one of his less bone jarring landings on the porchway entrance platform. Folding his wings neatly in alongside his flanks and with Binnie and Mira peering anxiously over his shoulders he strode boldly through the high archway of the portal and into the tower.

The trio found themselves in a large, bare, stone-lined room. The back of the room was partitioned off from the rest by a heavy wrought iron grill that went from floor to ceiling and wall to wall, mortared securely into the adjoining stonework. All that could be seen behind the grill was a rough hewn table, two basic stools and the open mouth of a stairwell that went down, to somewhere.

"I don't like this..."

With a loud and final sounding clang a heavy iron portcullis slammed down in the portal doorway. In the stunned silence that followed solid sounding locks could be heard clicking into place somewhere out of sight.

It was a huge cell and they were trapped!

Bizarh dashed to the portcullis, took a firm grip and heaved with all his strength. To no avail. Binnie flew from his scaly back in a panic and flitted around the cell looking for an opening small enough for an escape. Mira joined her, but there was no escape for the two of them either. The grills of iron were just the right size, or wrong size depending on which side of them one stood. The gaps were just too small for even the little forest creatures to squeeze through.

After several frenzied moments while each tried and failed, the pair resigned themselves to their situation. In search of inspiration they turned to Bizarh only to find him sitting glumly on the stone floor looking longingly out through the bars at the open sky beyond. With their wing beats sounding loud in the silence that surrounded them all, Little Binnie and Mira flew to the green dragon's side and sat down beside him.

"What now?" asked Binnie again, clearly terrified.

Again Bizarh shrugged.

A raucous, triumphant laugh sounded suddenly behind them and the three jerked in surprise. As one they spun.

Standing behind the bars at the back of the room, arms folded across his chest, stood a tall man. Actually, there were three people present although the two surly looking elves behind the laughing man drew little interest or attention. The three prisoners' eyes saw only the one. His presence seemed at once to dominate the entire room. Binnie and Mira darted straight behind Bizarh, who drew himself up to full sitting height in a bold gesture of his own, but didn't have nerve enough to approach the grill and the man beyond.

For this man really was quite magnificent, in a sinister sort of way.

The wizard, for that is what he undoubtedly was, was tall, as indeed all wizards are. But unlike any other of those who practised the magic arts, he was totally bereft of any facial hair. It was unusual enough that his chin was whisker free but the fact that his scalp was bare, pink and shiny was almost staggering. The Elfin people were naturally hairy so did he shave it? Or worse, had he actually used magic on himself to prevent it growing?

In the round puddle of pale flesh of his face burned two dark coals of fire that were his eyes. They didn't so much look at you as bore right into your soul. It was a glare powerful enough to pin down a person's spirit like a collector's specimen on a card inside a glass case. And his look seemed at that moment all the more chilling because of, rather than in spite of, the fact that he still laughed.

Wrapped about his shoulders was a cape of deepest black that fell in arrow straight folds to the floor at his feet. It had a high, stiff collar that encircled the back of his head, framing the pale whiteness of his face to great effect. And as if this weren't startling enough, the top of this curved collar was trimmed with an iridescent, shimmering, light catching frill. Moonglider wing! Even Bizarh knew that wearing a cloak thus decorated was not only very possibly illegal, but, more importantly, was a blatant affront to his majesty the King.

The wizard's only other visible garment could not hope to out dazzle the collar of the great cape but was not all that far behind it in its splendour. He wore flowing robes that swirled about his torso and also swept right down to the floor. They were in a deep two tone purple colour, splashed here and there with small embroideries of stars, moons and mystic symbols, worked into the cloth in what appeared to be real gold thread. The robes were drawn in at the waist by a linked gold belt with a great buckle at its centre, the buckle encrusted with blood red rubies and skilfully sculpted pieces of jet.

"Goth?" asked Bizarh in a small voice.

The wizard stopped laughing abruptly and raised one eyebrow. He acknowledged his name, bobbing his head in the tiniest of bows, and said evenly.

"You would have heard of me of course, but then I know of you too. Do you think I would be unprepared for your arrival? What do you think of my welcome?" He opened his arms wide to indicate their prison. His robes shimmered as they moved. When he received no answer he simply laughed again. "Speechless at my generosity, eh? Good. After all, you wouldn't want to offend me now, would you?" The words came out in a half-joke, half-threat. "Still, you can stay and enjoy my hospitality until I decide what to do with you all."

"But," Bizarh managed with difficulty to regain some of his composure. "We came here to see you because there is a great disaster going on in the forest even as we speak and..."

"SILENCE!" Goth's bark was not overly loud, but was simply and instantly obeyed, such was his power. "I have no interest in your miserable forest. You will remain my prisoner... guests." He flashed a fleeting, cold smile, "until I have decided what to do with you."

"Er... like... like what?"

Only just visible, peering tentatively over Bizarh's broad shoulder, Little Binnie had somehow found some of her courage and voice.

Goth's voice at once became soft, almost charming, but chilling. "Oh, I don't exactly know. I understand moonglider wings are extremely valuable and that cloud-hopper pelts are very, very soft. And as for a *green* dragon... well..." His laugh came again, loud and evil in the tower cell.

Instantly dismissing the forest dwellers he turned his back on the trio and said sternly to the two elves there, without even bothering to look directly at them. "Keep a close watch on them."

With that he flowed across the floor, at no time were his feet visible, and was disappearing down the stairwell before the two trembling turnkeys managed to blurt out.

"Er... yes... yes, Milord... we..."

He was gone.

The elves turned to face their prisoners, lowered themselves slowly onto the stools and commenced scowling in their direction.

In a quiet, terrified voice, Mira said simply.

"Oh, my..."

* * * * *

Blairoggin and his little companions flew on towards their destination in silence, all the time acutely aware of the ever shadowing presence of Agranth sliding effortlessly along at the Keeper of the Keys' wingtip.

The King's dragon always seemed to make full use of his imposing presence, simply by what he represented as much as with his sheer and impressive bulk. He easily matched the 'smaller' dragon with its unusual passengers, but that was by no means implying that Blairoggin was in anyway small himself. It was just that Agranth was simply huge.

The in-line formation crossed the forest canopy straight lining forwards on the bearing that Alcor had given them. They found themselves rapidly approaching their destination.

Kizzy paid little attention to their approaching destination, watching the King's dragon in awed, open-mouthed fascination. He flew with such grace, elegance and power it was indeed hard *not* to look at him. It was an almost magical combination and the cloud-hopper nodded in realisation as she understood that that was it. He was just majestic.

Alcor in contrast looked wholly content to sleep away the daylight hours in ignorant bliss, even though he said he would stay awake. It made little difference, he had given directions and knew they had only a short distance to go. So the moonglider passed the time in slumber, wings outspread towards the sun's rays looking like a small, iridescent saddle across Blairoggin's broad back.

And then they were there. They all saw it at once, a wide gap that appeared in the hinterland of the forest canopy and Blairoggin led the way, dipping lower and flying in to complete a full circuit of the green oasis. They all knew it by description even if they hadn't been there in person before. The castle with the tall white towers at the centre of the lawned gardens confirmed the location, as if that were really necessary.

The Whispering Spires.

Agranth continued to stay close on the Keeper of the Keys' wingtip as the pair circled in perfect formation. As much as the small herd of Unicorns gathered there on the ground looked up in slack-jawed amazement, so Agranth stared back down at the before unseen gathering of so many of the renowned shy beasts. But of course, he was much more discreet in his observations than those gaping from the ground, but still just as impressed. A brief smile crossed his firm jaw. This adventure just got better and better. Cearanth would be beside herself with jealousy when he told her.

The dragons of stature swept in low over the perimeter tree tops and with a soft whoosh of air glided deftly around the white spires, crossed the gardens beyond them and over the Unicorn herd before slowing to a stall and executing a perfect landing in the middle of the great lawn. Right up until they were motionless on the firm earth Agranth had kept perfect formation. By now Blairoggin thought the King's dragon was rather showing off.

After they had landed a silence fell across the whole area. The Unicorns, which Agranth had fully expected to see fleeing into the forest the moment they touched down, remained motionless, finding themselves now between the dragons and the castle. They appeared undecided as to any action at all and the silence deepened as no one seemed to want to make a move or utter a sound.

Then a tall Elf appeared at the entrance to the castle and began to make his way steadily across to the dragon pair. Agranth was again surprised as the Unicorns looked to this man without fear. In actual fact the King's dragon had only ever seen one Unicorn before and that had been from a distance, but he felt he knew all about them and their habits. Their timidness was virtually legendary. Yet what he was now witnessing didn't fit at all with what he thought he knew. The Unicorns gathered before him seemed to treat the Elf with some deference and parted without a sound to allow him free passage through their midst. The dragon pulled his gaze away from the spiral uni-horned beasts to focus his attention on the man who approached. Only then did he realise that the tall one was a wizard. Which might explain some of what was going on for strange things could happen around wizards, he knew.

The tall Elf stepped boldly up until he stood directly before the two, a soft smile on his rather cheery face. If nothing else, he certainly wasn't afraid.

Both dragons eyed him with great curiosity. He looked just how one might imagine a wizard should look. With a full, long beard almost as white as his spires, a tall pointed hat worn at a rather jaunty angle, and a long, full length robe with enormous, gaping cuffs at the ends of almost overlong sleeves. Quite impressive and imposing, but somehow not at all intimidating.

Yet the dragons knew they too were imposing and almost as one drew themselves up to full seated height, both presenting magnificent profiles. That was until Kizzy flitted into view and up onto Blairoggin's head and settled between his horns. The Keeper of the Keys suddenly felt robbed of much of his dragonly dignity.

If the blue dragon apparently was, it didn't register in the wizard's eyes. He beamed widely and when he finally spoke his voice carried a feeling of quiet strength and inner peace.

"Ah, a cloud-hopper. How absolutely charming." Then he bowed deeply to his visitors. "Welcome to The Whispering Spires. I am Oaken-Pel. How may I be of assistance?"

Agranth turned toward Blairoggin and smiled a smile that wasn't quite a smirk.

"Well, go on then."

With only a sideways glance back at the King's dragon Blairoggin took a deep breath and began to explain just why he and his companions had eventually ended up at The Whispering Spires. Oaken-Pel listened patiently, but Blairoggin could tell by his expression that the wizard thought his story a tall tale.

"And just how did this so called brownness come to exist?" interrupted the wizard after a short while.

"With the collision of the three spells."

"And you say that one of them is mine?"

"Yes."

"And that it is now a form of creeping death?"

"Yes!" Blairoggin's exasperation was quite apparent, much to the smug amusement of Agranth.

"Well, I'm sorry." Oaken-Pel was completely unperturbed by the big blue dragon's huff. "But I would never get even slightly involved with any kind of death spell. So you must be mistaken in your search for me."

Agranth nodded in agreement. Good, someone else sensible at last. Blairoggin swallowed. He suddenly had a nasty vision of himself clapped in irons and dragged in disgrace before the King. His voice held a sudden hint of desperation.

"But Naiouli said it should happen this way. Follow the aura and find the wizard."

"Naiouli?" Oaken-Pel's attitude changed abruptly. "Naiouli says she knows about this?"

"Yes. More I think than she lets on."

"Well why didn't you say so." He eyed the dragon keenly. "Well don't just stand there, tell me again, everything you know. And leave nothing out."

Now it was Agranth who looked unsure and watched in silence as the blue dragon beside him again explained all he knew about these strange goings on to the wizard, the tall Elf now giving his utmost attention. Oaken-Pel seemed particularly impressed with the fact that the little moongliders could see wizards' auras, making a mental note to have a little chat with Blairoggin's bright winged friend when he awoke.

"What is known of the other two spells?" he asked when the tale, what there was of it, was finally told.

"I don't know." Blairoggin shrugged. "I only know that Naiouli seems to be much more aware of the seriousness of the situation. I'm really nothing more than a messenger. If you want to find out more perhaps we should all go to see her at Unicorn Glade."

To Agranth's utter surprise Oaken-Pel immediately nodded in agreement. The wizard froze for a moment, apparently musing to himself over some deep thought. For a long moment silence again reigned among The Whispering Spires.

"Yes, yes. A sound idea," he finally said and nodded to himself again. "Naiouli eh? Yes, we must go as soon as possible." Then he

big as a building against an assault from a dragon. Such magic would take time and preparation while Decorum knew without doubt that he could reduce Tourmalane's precious building to nothing more than a pile of rubble in no time at all. And with the added bonus of having fun while doing it! But this was not his objective. Just a means to an end. Now he had the wizard it was time to soften the blow. He allowed himself a brief, private smile then turned back to face Tourmalane, his stern expression back in place.

"You're right. It isn't necessary. Because all I want from you is your undivided attention for a few days. It's simple. You come with me, help sort out the bother with this creeping brownness then return to your cosy castle, spell store untouched. I'll even supply the transport both ways. A couple of days, that's all. Look at it as a short break. Who knows, you might even find it interesting."

Tourmalane said nothing, glaring up at the dragon.

Matching the glare and without taking his eyes from those of the wizard, Decorum drew his tail high up over his back, twitched it to flick out the curved blades for added effect, then brought the powerful tail down hard and smashed it against the surface of the arch behind him. The ground tremored slightly under the blow and a few tiles slid down from the top of the store roof, dropped silently through the still air then clattered to the stony ground, smashing into jagged fragments.

Tourmalane held up his hands in surrender.

"All right. All right. I'll come with you..."

"Just as a goodwill gesture?" Decorum finished the sentence for him.

"Yes."

"Why thank you. So kind."

With a flourish of his arms Tourmalane threw an exaggerated bow, making the gesture match the amount of sarcasm as was in Decorum's words.

"I'll get my travelling bag." He turned and moved in through the castle gate, only going a few paces before pulling up and saying over his shoulder, "I'll only be a few minutes, I promise. Don't do anything rash." There was a brief pause before he added. "Please?"

Decorum flashed him a fanged smile and bowed in acknowledgement. Without another word the wizard disappeared from sight into the castle.

The Gate Keeper sat down and the smile settled into a self satisfied grin. He rather liked this 'You've got a big stick, I've got an even bigger stick' diplomacy.

Perhaps he had discovered within himself a new found talent.

Sirus and Zoozie would have been impressed.

UNICORN GLADE
PHOEBE MOON
1997

6

A Kind Of Magic

Blairoggin and Agranth were once again on the wing. This time flying side by side as they covered the relatively short distance, as the carrion bird flies, between the Whispering Spires and Unicorn Glade.

Blairoggin looked across at the King's dragon, smiling to see his companion still appear as majestic as ever, even with Oaken-Pel sitting at the very top of his broad shoulders, legs doing their best to straddle the base of the dragon's neck. Agranth noticed the expression and smiled back. He was supremely competent and yet careful with his passenger, keeping within the limitations he had learned long ago when taking the King on his flights. His Majesty enjoyed flying, getting aloft as often as he could to savour the freedom and relief from his royal duties, as much as Agranth did from getting the opportunity just to get airborne and fly simply for flying's sake. Even Kizzy and Alcor rode comfortably in their travel, both considering themselves now somewhat seasoned dragon flyers. It was Oaken-Pel who was unsure. The sky was not the natural habitat of an Elf as far as he was concerned. But with a stoic acceptance that needs must, he suffered in silence, beard flailing over one shoulder in the slipstream. His arms gripped his spell book as tightly as his legs gripped the base of the Agranth's neck and he steadfastly refused to even glance groundwards, his eyes locked firmly on the line of the distant horizon.

The forest canopy below suddenly seemed to part and the dragon pair swept into a wide arc, giving all the passengers who cared to look a panoramic view of Unicorn Glade, the small herd of Unicorns gathered in one corner of it and the elegant castle of Naiouli the mystic. Agranth raised an eye ridge in surprise at the sight of even more unicorns, noting as he flew by that a few of them

Naiouli's home and a haven for Unicorns.

were actually winged. Although his Unicorn knowledge had earlier been called into question, he knew for certain that only the older beasts grew wings and were very rarely seen by *anyone*, two or four legged. Things simply got better and better!

Blairoggin of course had seen all this before and appeared indifferent to the rare sight below him. Agranth kept his growing respect for the Keeper of the Keys hidden and together the dragons manoeuvred for approach, came in slow and low over the trees and settled gently down, well gently for two great dragons of stature, onto the lush grass in the middle of the Glade.

Agranth dipped his head low and Oaken-Pel stumbled gratefully to the ground, tucked his spell book tight under his arm and stood silently before the dragon pair. The King's dragon sent a puzzled look across at Blairoggin, but was dissuaded from asking the question by a swift shake of his companion's head. The cloud-hopper atop it swayed expertly to stay on and there followed a long moment of silence before all heads turned towards the castle. Just a moment before Agranth had been sure there was no one in sight, but now he watched in mute admiration as the most beautiful Elfin girl he had ever seen, who seemed to have appeared as if by magic, was suddenly there in front of the main gate. She was a true vision of loveliness, and he should know as he'd seen many true beauties paraded before the King in the days when his Royal Highness was Elysia's most eligible man. The Elfin beauty made her way across the lushness of the Glade towards the waiting group. Made her way because she didn't appear to actually walk as far as those watching could see. Agranth cocked his massive head, but even his sensitive hearing could not detect the sound of any footsteps. Her long white robe flowed both down to the ground and elegantly out behind her as she moved, the gossamer cloth totally hiding her feet. If she did indeed stride then her pace was so even that she did not bounce. It was as if she simply floated effortlessly across the surface of the green earth, passing by yet somehow not quite touching it. A mesmerising sight. Even so, Agranth was still aware in his peripheral vision of all the Unicorns moving in on either side of the two dragons, their attentions also focused on the Elf woman. She stopped before them all, gazing at them with an effortless intensity.

Oaken-Pel bowed very low, as did Blairoggin and Agranth found himself following suit.

"Naiouli," said the wizard warmly. "It is truly a great pleasure to see you once again." Naiouli offered out a smile that warmed the heart. Oaken-Pel drank in the sight, as did everyone else, then continued as if there had been no delightful interruption. "But if what this blue dragon here says is true, then I am sorry my visit is not under better circumstances."

Then came the most amazing thing for Agranth. He heard the woman's soft, sweet tones as clear as day, yet not once did she appear to open her mouth.

You are wise, as always Oaken-Pel. It is indeed good to see you. Her eyes lifted to the giant beasts behind him. *And my good dragon and his little friends. And this, I assume, is the great Agranth, blood dragon to His Majesty the King?*

Agranth jerked in realisation that her attention had focused on him. He realised he had been staring.

"Er... yes madam. I... er... am glad to make your acquaintance."

Thank you. She smiled and he couldn't help it, he smiled back. *I am glad you are here, for I have a task for you, if you would be so kind.*

Agranth just nodded without even thinking, spellbound.

Blairoggin leaned over until their heads were quite close together. He smiled at his friend's sudden tameness.

"Don't be too shocked," he whispered. "She affects us all like that. Wonderful, isn't it?"

Thank you my good dragon. Naiouli bowed at the compliment and, of course, Blairoggin couldn't help it. He bowed back.

"Yes, yes." Oaken-Pel interrupted, apparently unaffected by Naiouli's magnificence. "But is it true? About the creeping brownness and how us wizards are responsible?"

Yes, but do not blame yourselves. You were not to know and it is all the result of unfortunate timing. There is much to do my friend and I will explain all that I know but first we must ensure that we are ready.

"Ready for what?" Agranth whispered to Blairoggin. The Keeper of the Keys just shrugged in reply.

Naiouli turned once again to Agranth.

I cannot reveal all to you at this time, but it is enough that you know we need all Elysia's dragons of stature here if catastrophe is to be averted.

"Catastrophe?" Agranth thought this a rather large word to describe a smallish patch of brown dead plants.

Without any more mindwords, though as if in direct reply to Agranth's unspoken thoughts, Naiouli beckoned forward a winged Unicorn with an impressively tightly spiralled horn.

"I am Crystal," said the remarkable creature softly, knowing that no further explanation would be necessary. Then she looked up into Agranth's crystalline eyes, locked their gazes together and in a fleeting moment showed the great dragon in his mind's eye what would happen if the creeping brownness went unchecked. It was a rare display of one of Crystal's lesser known talents. Not quite sure what was going on, for an instant Blairoggin thought he detected a flash of fear pass across the dragon's features but he couldn't be sure. Then Crystal bowed and looked away. Agranth looked back at Naiouli, simply speechless.

She did not smile.

So you see, what I ask I do not ask lightly. Please, go at once to Talla-Weyre. Tell the King what has already happened here and that you must return with Cearanth.

"I will do whatever I can," said Agranth gravely. "But I cannot predict what the King will say or do. What if he does not permit it?"

I would never ask you to disobey your King, but I feel he will not deny you your request. Trust me.

And without question, he did.

"Then I shall go at once."

He bowed deeply to all there and everyone bowed in return. A wave of sudden pride rose within him, pride at being even a small part of what was now without doubt the greatest adventure in the history of Elysia. He turned to Blairoggin, who had brought him into this event.

"Be well, Keeper of the Keys," he said warmly, and held out one huge fisted paw. Without hesitation Blairoggin butted his own fist against it.

"See you soon, my friend."

"Count on it." He grinned widely then coiled and launched straight up into the blue.

Bizarh had now been sitting for several hours, still glumly looking out through his prison bars at the cheerless, mist-shrouded view beyond.

Mira, unable any longer to fight his natural urges, had sought out what he considered to be the safest spot, Bizarh's back, and finally fallen asleep. His spread wings looked lacklustre in the absence of any sunshine.

Little Binnie had paced about the floor and flown around the entire room for a while, all the time trying to find some way out, before at last settling down in defeat beside her big green friend. Even so her head continued to flick back and forth, eyes checking the outside scene and the sour faced Elfin guards opposite.

"We've just got to get out of here," she said rather unnecessarily.

"I know." The dejection in Bizarh's voice was painfully obvious. "But we must also somehow get Goth to come with us back to Unicorn Glade."

Binnie surprised herself by managing to laugh out loud. "We'll be lucky if we even live long enough to see the black wizard again."

Bizarh looked reproachfully down at the cloud-hopper and her head dropped. There was no need for extra scaremongering. They were already frightened enough and she knew that despite their fears Bizarh was still seeing the bigger picture. There was more than just their own lives at stake here. The big dragon had a big heart and she drew some warmth from being with him. Looking back up she changed tack.

"Are you sure you can't break through these bars?"

Bizarh simply nodded.

"Even with your great strength?"

"Even with my great strength."

The cloud-hopper looked for a long moment at the heavy bars then straight into Bizarh's eye.

"Could you break through them if you changed to bronze again?"

This time it was Bizarh who managed a laugh.

"You'd know that better than me. I don't remember all that much about what happened the last time. Or even how I managed to change in the first place."

"But you do remember some of it?" Binnie thought she saw a glimmer of hope.

"Well, a little." Bizarh pondered for a moment. "I knew what I needed to do. I mean, I knew I had to get out. No matter how, I had to get out. That much is certainly clear."

Binnie nodded thoughtfully.

"Well, all you need to remember this time is that we must all get out." There was a pause before she added. "And when, if, we go, we must take Goth with us."

Bizarh nodded emphatically in agreement and was about to reply when he saw his little friends brow furrowed in deep thought. The words remained unsaid and Bizarh found himself looking down in sudden admiration at the thinking, planning cloud-hopper before him. Times had certainly changed, he realised.

Perhaps Little Binnie now wasn't quite so little after all.

Decorum flew back across the expanse of green landscape that lay spread out before him, the jagged mountains of the Great Range at his back, already receding. Perched on his back sat the sullen, but not unappreciative Tourmalane.

There was from the outset undeniable confidence in the posture the wizard had adopted as he sat astride the base of the Gate Keeper's neck. But as the flight progressed the tall Elf's resolve gradually softened and he settled into a more relaxed position. Even he couldn't deny the fact that despite his earlier complaints he was now rather enjoying himself.

Not many people, he didn't really consider four legged creatures as real people, ever got to fly on a dragon's back. In fact he doubted he could count the number on the fingers of one hand. Only their royal majesties the King and Queen readily came to mind among the chosen few. His surprise therefore when they had stopped *en route* to pick up a moonglider and a cloud-hopper was undisguised. This surprise was further compounded by the friendly way they spoke, as if in partnership, the tiny forest dwellers speaking to this giant, powerful beast as an equal.

Tourmalane turned his head and looked down at his fellow passengers now. The moonglider of course slept, beautiful wings outstretched before the sun. The cloud-hopper, who had earlier falteringly introduced herself as Zoozie before lapsing into a timid silence, now looked up as she felt his gaze and offered the wizard a half-smile. At no time though did she shift from her low, crouching, aerodynamic position, nose forward into the wind.

Sensible, he thought, gave the briefest nod of acknowledgement in return then also resumed his own aerodynamic position. After a little experimentation he had found that by resting his arms across the travelling bag on his lap and by leaning into the slipstream he could relax while the air pressure took most of his weight. He realised also after a while that a rather pleasant grin had settled easily on his face.

"Where are we going?" he shouted at Decorum over the dragon's neck.

The Gate Keeper never even glanced back.

"Unicorn Glade," came the gruff reply. "Be there before the day is out."

"Then what?"

The replying shrug almost caused Tourmalane to lose his bag from his lap. A frantic snatch saved it from a long drop and he took a firmer grip on it, opened his mouth to shout back a complaint, then thought the better of it. Leaning forward once more into the slipstream he too gave a shrug. After all what was the point? He couldn't exactly get off now, could he? He settled down once more in silence, accepting the fact that he'd simply have to wait and see what happened when the time came. For now it seemed right just to enjoy the flying.

It wasn't long before he found that pleasantly silly grin back on his face once more.

* * * * *

Binnie suddenly noticed movement on the other side of the barrier, at the back of their tower room prison. The two Elfin guards appeared all at once restless, a complete contrast to their, until now, silent and virtually motionless vigil. Even their scowls had seemed frozen in place. But they now twitched to the alert and it was Bizarh's sensitive ears that also picked up the sound of distant footsteps, trudging invisibly up the stairwell. The forest dwellers froze in terror.

The two Elves jumped on the instant to their feet, adapting what they considered a stand to attention, only to slump back into a slouch as another pair of Elves appeared. This pair looked just as surly as the first only one carried a heavy looking sack made of a coarsely woven fibre.

"Get away," grunted the empty handed Elf of the second pair. "Our turn. Go get some grub."

Without a second bidding the relieved Elves made for the stairs. One thumbed over his shoulder at the prisoners behind the grill. "No problem," he hissed. "They're shakin' in their boots." And with that vanished down the staircase.

The new guards looked at their prisoners, saw the truth and scoffed before turning away and sitting opposite each other at the rough table.

Bizarh and Binnie knew that truth too. If Goth was dragging out their fate just to make them sweat, he was succeeding! But they took time to examine these new Elves. They were as rough and ready as their first turnkeys, the only difference being that they paid little if no attention at all to their charges. As they watched, the Elf with the sack plonked it down on the table, opened the neck and reached in. First he produced a pair of leather mugs, then a corked earthenware flagon. Next came two flat wooden plates, a heavy, stodgy looking loaf, some strong smelling cheese and a wicked looking, jagged bladed knife. It proved to be sharp too as the Elf carved off a few slices of cheese then hacked some lumps off the loaf. The second Elf uncorked the flagon and filled both mugs, replacing the bung with a concerted thump.

For the second time in her life Binnie smelled a distinctive odour, one that right now held a slight whiff of hope. She looked at Bizarh for a long moment, then eyed again the drinkers, settling back to give them both her full attention. Bizarh caught the cloud-hopper's mood, if not her intentions, and also settled down to watch, the pair now scrutinising the feasting guards with an unblinking gaze.

It didn't take too long, they were clearly tough, but also just as clearly not the brightest Elves in the kingdom of Elysia.

After holding out for a brief spell against the intrusive viewing one of the Elves shot a sideways glance at the pair. He quickly looked away again, only holding out for a short while longer against the continuous stares. Finally he turned on his stool to face his antagonisers.

"What !" he barked, showing a bit of temper.

Bizarh and Binnie kept silent.

After a moment both Elves put down their food and looked at their prisoners. One rather too casually rested a hand on the nasty looking club at his belt.

"Well?" The same Elf again.

Bizarh, still none the wiser to Binnie's idea, stepped back to let her lead off. As if in complete obedience to the green dragon, the cloud-hopper dutifully trotted across to the metal grid between the two parties. Both Elves moved cautiously back against the far wall, hands reaching for their clubs.

Binnie had to stifle a smile.

"Do not be afraid," she said cheerily. "I'm just the messenger."

"We're not afraid," barked the lead Elf.

"No," agreed the second on the instant. "We're just being ready. Don't know what you're up to but it won't work. You'll get no change from us. We ain't even got the key to your cage so don't bother."

"We don't want the key," said Binnie casually. Bizarh looked on in astonishment. As did the Elves.

"You don't?"

Binnie shook her head, then flicked it to indicate the dragon still sitting by the barred portal.

"It's him. My master. I don't know if you know, but dragons have to drink a lot. All the time. I think it's something to do with that fire they carry inside them."

Not too bright at all. Both Elves scowled briefly at Bizarh before one said, "Really?"

The other thumped his partner in the ribs and said gruffly, "So?"

"So... you wouldn't want your master to come back later and find he's captured a sick, maybe even a dying dragon now, would you?"

Bizarh had to work hard just to stop his huge jaw from gaping open at that. The Elves jaws did instead.

"Huh?" said one.

"Dying?" said the other.

Binnie nodded emphatically. "He just needs a drink. To sort of tide him over. The mighty Goth wouldn't be best pleased to find his prize catch in poor condition when he returns. And just who do you s'pose he'll take it out on if he finds a dead dragon in his cage?"

As realisation slowly overtook the Elves they looked at one another and the colour drained from their faces. Fear showed on their pug features before one replaced it with a scowl and said gruffly.

"You can't scare us," he lied. "He told us just to watch you. Nuffing more."

"And you can watch the dragon die if you like. But is that what Goth would like? All the dragon wants is a drink. I promise we won't do anything. Besides, like you said, you haven't got the key. What would be the point?"

The Elves looked undecidedly at each other. It was plain even to Bizarh that they were weighing up the options of surrendering a drink or doing nothing and facing the possible consequences if what the cloud-hopper was telling them was true. The green dragon slowly lowered his head, let his shoulders sag and tried to put on what he thought was a hangdog expression. Binnie saw the overacting and so hurriedly pushed her advantage.

"Just a small drink. A cupful. Like I said, to tide him over. A simple cupful can't hurt now, can it?"

There was a long, agonising moment of indecision.

"We ain't got no water."

"That's OK," said Binnie casually. "Anything wet will do fine."

The pair thought some more then nodded. The lead Elf said to his partner. "You get right back and be ready in case they try anything. I'll shove a mug on the floor through the bars." His partner just nodded. "Right you are." He pointed at Binnie with his now drawn club. "Get back against the window with your green pal."

The cloud-hopper bowed deeply and flew back to Bizarh's side, settled and tried to adopt a casual pose. Everyone watched in silence as the Elf poured a full mug of liquid from the flagon, placed it on the floor at the base of the bars and carefully pushed it through with the end of his club. Then he beat a hasty retreat to join his second at the back of the tower.

Binnie flew back to the bars and peered into the mug.

"Thank you so much. My master will be so pleased," she said as sincerely as she could then gripped the rim of the mug tightly in her teeth and very carefully carried it across the cell. She put it gently down on the floor in front of Bizarh. Eyeing the liquid, she hoped it would be enough.

Bizarh lowered his head until they were almost eye to eye.

"I can't believe what you just said," he whispered. "What a pack of lies! We dragons can go for weeks without a drink. And as for me being your master..."

"Yes, but they don't know that. Anyway, it's not to quench your thirst. I just hope there's enough."

"Enough what?"

Binnie sniffed at the liquid. "Elvengrog."

"For what?" Bizarh still had no idea what she had in mind.

Binnie checked to see that although the Elves were watching they couldn't hear, then looked her friend in the eye.

"Look. I think this is the stuff that set you off last time. You know, in the tavern, when you changed."

"Really?" Bizarh looked now into the mug with bright fascination.

"Yes, but you have to help. Tell me, what do you remember about that. The last thing you recall before everything went hazy?"

Bizarh furrowed his brow.

"Well... Fire. Yes, fire. Hot. Inside me. I felt on fire all the way from the top of my head to the tip of my tail."

"And that's what you've got to think of now. Try and make yourself feel hot inside, yes?"

"Well..."

Binnie tried not to sound too desperate. "It might be our only chance to get out of here."

Bizarh nodded. "I'll try."

Binnie smiled. "Good. But before all that you must remember above all one thing and one thing only."

Bizarh raised his eye ridges.

"You must remember to go to Unicorn Glade and to take Goth with you. Say it now."

"Go to Unicorn Glade and take Goth with me. "Bizarh dutifully recited the line, past trying to fathom out his little friend's reasoning.

"Now, close you eyes and *think* it. Several times."

Bizarh did as he was told.

"Got it," he said finally.

"Right!" Binnie gave one more glance at the still silently

watching Elves then flew up onto the green dragon's back. "Just let me get a good grip. I hope Mira doesn't fall off." Noting with satisfaction the moonglider's deep slumbers she checked her purchase one more time. "Now, my good friend, what are we going to do?"

"Go to Unicorn Glade and take Goth with me," said Bizarh loudly.

"Right!" Binnie's voice was loud now too. "Now drink, and think hot."

The green dragon nodded, ignoring the astonished looks of the guards who were witnessing a tiny cloud-hopper shouting orders at a dragon of stature.

Then Bizarh dipped his massive head, gripped the rim of the mug deftly between his lips, inhaled deeply through his nose and with a flick of his head tossed the mug's liquid contents straight into the back of his throat.

There was a sudden, strange, strained silence as everyone there voluntarily froze, waiting for something to happen, not knowing just what or even if it would but somehow filled with expectancy.

Bizarh squeezed his eyes tight shut and thought hot. And found it easy because it simply was. The potent elvengrog burned his throat and on down into his stomach. The strangest thing was that it was as if part of his being was willing itself to be hot. Positive thought did help this will and Bizarh experienced deep within himself a great pleasure and release at the expansion of feeling within him. The elvengrog was but the spark. The green dragon's co-operative will fanned the flame and heat roared through his body, lighting him up from within, from the tip of his long tail right up his neck until it thundered inside his brain. Sensing success, the small part of Bizarh's mind that remained independently cognitive shouted out above the roar, 'Unicorn Glade and take Goth!'

On Bizarh's back, Binnie felt a great tremor shake the green dragon. The scales on his back where she held on seemed to fizz beneath her little hooves. Then all the great scales across his back eclipsed and turned a dark shade of hard, metallic bronze. Out of the corner of her eye she glimpsed the guard Elves stagger back until they were flat against the far wall.

One gasped out loud. “Oh, Drok!”

Then Binnie felt herself rise as Bizarh seemed to physically grow in stature beneath her. Even Mira came awake with a jolt and the pair clung on for grim life as the dragon they rode bulged in a ripple of power-filled muscle. His wings enlarged and thickened and a deep roar burst from their friend’s throat.

Driven by his recently impressed urge to get out and go where he’d been told, Bizarh lumbered up to the portal exit barred by the metal portcullis. He gripped the bars tightly, let out a tremendous bellow as he exerted pressure, and pulled. The metal screeched in protest against the stress then shredded in Bizarh’s paws like so many strands of wet parchment. At the sight of this the Elf guards fled for their lives, fleeing down the stairwell and shouting for their lord Goth at the top of their lungs.

With a final swipe of his fist the warp dragon Bizarh smashed away the last twisted strands of the portcullis and leaped straight out into the void, Binnie and Mira almost being jerked free from their perches by the sudden burst of acceleration. In a matter of moments they were circling the tower in a great loop, the watery sun glinting off the bronze scales of Bizarh’s enlarged body.

Wizard Goth had been immediately alerted to the fact that something untoward had happened, as much by the sounds of rending metal as by the loud and terrified cries of his Elfin minions. It just so happened that his private chambers were also within the tall tower, further down below the prison room. At the sounds of commotion and panic he leapt to his feet and dashed to the nearest windows, flung them wide and stepped out onto the small balcony beyond it. To his utter amazement he looked up to see a great battle dragon swooping into view from behind the tower he now occupied. Where the beast had come from he had no idea.

Almost at the same moment Binnie saw the wizard too.

“Look...” she shouted but needn’t have bothered. Bizarh, even in his warped state, also recognised the wizard and without hesitation vectored in on the tall, black clad Elf.

Goth saw the beasts approach and drew back his hands, clenched them into fierce claws and with a dramatic lunge threw magic at him.

Now, it is an old Elysian saying that one can tell a lot about the general demeanour of a wizard by the ready magic he keeps up his sleeve. Great spells need time and preparation, but ready magic, to be done 'off the cuff' is a trademark of wizardry, commonly practised to impress lesser beings or to entertain visitors or friends. Most wizards can produce straight out of thin air something along the lines of bunches of flowers, instant rainbows, small amounts of gold coins or even the rather old cliché of a long-eared white rabbit. It all depends on the wizard's temperament as to what he usually kept, ready prepared, up his sleeve.

Without a moment's hesitation Goth launched a small orb of ball lightning at the now diving dragon. If not lethal then at least incapacitating, the compact jolt of electricity crackled up through the air and struck Bizarh on the right wing, close to where it joined the shoulder. The wizard's cry of triumph died on his lips as Bizarh took the blow with little more than a quiver, and dove straight at his attacker. Goth's claw hands turned into a feeble barrier as he raised them to protect his face.

Bizarh swooped, snatching the wizard up in his front paws, having to fly so close to the face of the tower that he inadvertently struck it with the leading edge of one wing as he passed. Reinforcing his grip on the wizard by using his rear paws too, Goth was drawn tight up against Bizarh's underbelly, finding himself encased from neck to ankles in the curled talons of the dragon. Totally immobile, it was all he could do to take a backward glance at his castle as his captor flew away. It was a brief glance, but with time enough to see the tall tower, the stonework knocked clean out above his balcony by Bizarh's strike, quiver once at its loss of support. The last image of his home was the terrible sight of the tower pitching forward to crash down as stone rubble, debris and dust onto the courtyard and walls below.

"To Unicorn Glade!" shouted Binnie, caught up in the excitement now she was free. "Unicorn Glade!"

Mira nodded in agreement, unable to speak, so stunned was he by the sudden violence and destruction.

Goth was also speechless, while an unnoticing Bizarh quickly eyed the position of the sun, took his bearings then headed back out across the lake and marshlands. With each powerful beat of his wings his speed increased. Within a few moments Binnie and Mira had to crouch very low on their friend's back to fight against the drag as they accelerated. The slipstream threatened to tear them off the bronze scales and Goth, still clutched tight beneath the dragon, found himself having to gasp for breath as the air blasted against his bare face.

Then, finding from somewhere an extra hidden reserve of power, Bizarh lunged forward and the speed of travel increased even more until the air that pushed against them all was almost unbearable. Just when they thought they could hold on no more there was an almost audible, sudden pop, everyone feeling as if they had somehow been physically pushed through an unseen barrier. Like falling through the skin of some huge drum. And the dragging slipstream was instantly gone!

The air close around Bizarh's body was calm and quiet. As one Binnie and Mira sat cautiously up, expecting at any moment to be snatched away by the wind. Then they crept forward and peered over the great dragon's shoulder and looked down, agog, at the ground below. It was flashing past now at a simply incredible rate! So fast in fact that the tree top canopy directly under them seemed to merge into a green blur. Even Goth forgot his predicament and gaped open-mouthed, his downward view unrestricted.

Bizarh, although still in spasm, also managed to feel the rush of discovery and take in the thrill of his warping along above the Elysian forest.

Binnie, aghast at the astounding velocity, turned to say as much to Mira but found the moonglider looking behind, at the way they had come. Binnie looked too. The castle, the lake that surrounded it, the marshlands and its damp mists were almost gone from sight, already far away towards the distant horizon. And still Mira stared.

"What... what do you see?" asked Binnie, her whisper loud and clear in the still air. "What is it?"

Mira knew that only he could see the trailing, ribbon-like green aura that was flowing out behind them. A small smile crossed his face.

"It's a kind of magic," was all he said.

Flowers and dragons, Flowerdragons.

7
Plans And Schemes

There was no denying the warm glow Agranth felt as he approached Talla-Weyre. The sight of the walled capital of Elysia always filled him with pleasure, but the sudden notion that all this glory might be under threat tempered the thought and he quickly brought his feelings back under control and his mind focused on the job in hand.

His renewed determination stopped him taking time to do his usual flypast of the city. Normally he considered it his duty to be fully visible as the representative of His Majesty the King, and in truth allow the populous to get a glimpse of his own magnificence, but now he flew straight in on a bearing directly to the castle. Executing a perfect stall at the entrance to his castle portal he landed lightly on the entrance plinth of his own room. Once inside he settled himself in his luxuriously padded, specially made nest. Knowing his approach would have been announced at once to His Majesty, he waited patiently to be summoned before his master.

It didn't take long.

A little, neatly dressed Elfin surf scurried in, didn't stand any nearer the huge, intimidating dragon than was necessary and after bowing said breathlessly.

"His Royal Majesty awaits you at your earliest convenience."

Meaning that he should go at once, Agranth nodded then flashed a tremendous, almost leering fang filled smile at the nervous serf. The Elf had vanished out the door even before the smile had reached full stretch and Agranth swore he could almost see the vapour trail left by the speed of the poor soul's departure.

He instantly flew back out of his lair, circled the castle once to settle his wings then flew straight in through the entrance to the royal chambers. Completing yet another perfect landing he carefully pulled in his wings, allowed himself a brief check to see that his appearance was acceptable, then stepped forward to present himself before their Royal Majesties.

The King's face was a picture of confusion. He wanted to know what was going on. The Queen's in contrast was more relaxed, knowing that all things would come clear in good time. They made the perfect, complementary couple and their falling deeply in love with each other had been without doubt the greatest stroke of good fortune ever to befall Elysia in recent times.

"Your Majesty." Agranth bowed low.

"My friend." The King jumped energetically to his feet. "I welcome your safe return, but am told you came back alone. I know you would not fail me, so what has happened?"

"Much, my liege. And there is much more to do. Also, I now know why two of your most trusted subjects have," he paused, "*appear* to have deserted their posts. Let me tell you now what I know."

Which he did.

At the finish the King and Queen sat speechless, both gaping open-mouthed in a quite un-royal like way, his Majesty slumping back down into his chair beside his wife.

"But... but what is to be done?"

It was the Queen who finally asked the big question, as Agranth had expected. As he also knew that the King would feel no need to correct or admonish his wife for her break of protocol and speaking for him. It was already done and besides, His Royal Highness knew he had the final say and that, more to the point, it was not the question, but the answer, that was all important. Wise, benevolent and aware of the importance of others around him, it was one of the attributes that made him such a good King. Qualities Agranth was now also becoming aware of among his own dragon fraternity. He allowed himself a small smile. This suddenly apparent parallel made him re-affirm his own closeness to the great Elf who sat before him and he felt very proud of his blood link with him.

"Yes," agreed the King, blissfully unaware of his dragon's admiration for him. "And Niaouli, she has already begun gathering those who would help, at Unicorn Glade? What is her plan?"

Agranth could not answer fully for he did not know what would happen at the end of it all. Who in Elysia did?

"All I know for certain is that she is gathering all the dragons of stature together. I believe they, we, are in some way crucial to the whole event. That is why she has sent me to ask you for your permission to return to Unicorn Glade, and to take Cearanth with me."

He held his breath. What was said next might in the long run finally determine the outcome of Naiouli's scheme. And perhaps also the eventual fate of all Elysia.

"Of course!" chorused the King and Queen as one.

"And of course we will accompany our dragons on this most vital of journeys," added the King with much gravity in his voice. The Queen nodded her beautiful head in agreement. Agranth's heart soared with relief and pride, one eye ridge also going up with surprise at the news of this unexpected Royal accompaniment. What an adventure!

Her Majesty rose to her feet and approached the great dragon.

"You have done well, our loyal friend."

"Here, here!" cheered the King from behind her.

Then, when the Queen was close enough to Agranth for her husband not to hear her, she whispered up at him.

"And Cearanth will be so pleased to be involved."

Agranth offered the wonderful woman before him a great fanged grin and, turning his head slightly so the eye nearest the Queen was obscured from the King's vision, winked the crystalline orb at her.

Not knowing that the royal house was awaiting her return, Cearanth made her way back towards Talla-Weyre in her own sweet time. She had thoroughly enjoyed her patrol over the lightly populated hinterlands of the city, flying with effortless grace and consummate skill above the little hamlets and field systems. It was a joy to be out and about as the royal symbol, the place usually taken by Agranth. While he was off gallivanting around the kingdom on his little 'adventure' she intended to take full advantage of the chance to be, at least for a while, top dragon of the city. Too often she had played second fiddle to the King's dragon, knowing full well she was his equal. Well here was a golden opportunity and she intended to make the most of it.

The Elves below her toiling at the soil seemed to think her a good representative. They all stopped and stared up at her as she flew past. And why shouldn't they? She was well worth a look.

Those who stared looked as much to see a female dragon of stature as much as for anything else. She dragons were, at least to those with an appreciative eye, subtly different to their male counterparts. Female dragons were more narrow in girth, but longer in the neck and seemed gifted at birth with more natural poise. Agranth was gold and magnificent. Cearanth was silver and elegant. Effortlessly so. It was difficult to explain, but even her flying technique was different. The same speeds and control in the air that made dragons of stature such a sight to behold were somehow achieved with a ladylike grace. Perhaps it was the more flowing, almost continuous sweeping wing beat, or the way her neck naturally adopted a majestic, swan like 'S' shape. The end result was a curious yet complete living picture of sleekness, elegance, power and presence. Those Elves in the royal court knew full well how perfectly the she dragon reflected the qualities of her mistress, the Queen.

Cearanth thought those who observed her passing were naturally friendly. The truth was that those who spied her beauty found a smile coming naturally to their faces, whether they intended it to or not. Was it not the famous Elfin philosopher Jonk Eets who once said :

'A thing of beauty is a joy forever.'

It is a common belief among the rank and file of Elysia that the said philosopher was looking at Cearanth when he composed that line.

The she dragon flew in through her own portal high up in the castle wall and had barely settled in her soft nest when a neat looking Elfin messenger appeared at speed, disturbing several of the silken drapes that hung from the surrounding walls. He bowed deeply, unavoidably smiling at the sight of the great creature before him. She lay coiled like a monstrous yet elegant winged cat upon an outrageously large satin cushion.

"Her Royal Highness begs your attendance in the flying room as soon as you are sufficiently rested."

An urgent royal summons. Cearanth's already high spirits soared some more. A definite prospect of even more fun and games.

"Tell the Queen that I will be there at once," she said softly. She rarely spoke any other way.

The Elf nodded and stood back among the soft drapes, not leaving immediately. He wanted, liked, to watch Cearanth take off if the chance to do so arose. It just looked so, well, good.

The Queen's dragon effortlessly uncoiled, appeared to skate across the chamber floor to the portal and flowed out into the clear air. There was no other word for it. She made the transition from land to air seem as natural as the sun going in and out behind clouds. Different facets of the same thing.

"Nice," said the still smiling Elf to himself and took the warm glow of appreciation with him to his next task.

Cearanth flew out over the courtyard then swooped back in towards the building and straight in through the flying room portal. This vast room resembled a hangar, with ample space for several dragons to land, move freely around and take off with ease. She landed easily, surprised to see Agranth already there. Along with their highnesses the King and Queen.

"Your Majesties." She bowed low. "Agranth," she added out of the corner of her mouth. The big gold dragon just grinned.

"My beautiful dragon," welcomed the Queen enthusiastically. "You will be glad I'm sure to know that we are going on a flight."

Cearanth had already surmised as much, for both their Majesties stood before her in full flying gear.

The King's was rather plain for someone of such a high status but spoke volumes of his flying experience, the more knowledgeable eye noting the simple, neat, business like professionalism of his attire. He wore sturdy calf-length leather boots with silver side buckles. Thick leather trousers, a trifle baggy in the knee and backside which showed they were the veterans of long flying hours, a great fur-lined leather jacket with a dazzling white fleece collar and gauntlets with silver finger ends and knuckle protectors. A beautiful charmworm silk scarf was knotted at his throat. On his head he wore a leather skull cap. Small copies of dragon wings fashioned in silver were attached over the ears and around his neck hung loose a pair of flying goggles, the lens rims and adjusters also of silver.

By contrast the Queen's outfit was just as efficient at deflecting the cold air, but showed rather more style. Her boots came to just above the knee and had short tassels sewn down the outside seam. He trousers were in black leather and rather expertly cut to show off her very good figure, tight in at the waist and with criss-crossing lacing down the outside of the thighs. Her jacket was thick and fur-lined against the slipstream, but stylishly double-breasted and had a waist belt, jauntily knotted to one side. Her gloves were thinner and more elegant than her husband's. Her helmet had several colourful swirler bird plumes sewn into the crown in such a way as to make them sweep out behind her. Rather than the King's flying goggles her hat had a broad silver band around it which held in place a wrap around face visor of wafer thin slymcrystal. This face protection was actually a section of the inner lining from a dragon egg. It was completely clear, as hard to damage as ironstone and difficult to obtain in decent sized pieces. It was a wonderful thing in itself but did its best not to hide any of the beauty of the lady smiling safely behind it.

She clapped her hands and a number of well turned out servants scurried forward carrying a pair of dragon saddles. These were virtually large, well padded buckets with leg holes and restraining belts for the occupants, and long leather straps to enable them to be buckled around the dragon's chest and neck. But the servants didn't dash forwards to strap the saddles onto the two winged beasts. Any dragon rider worth their salt always saddled his or her own mount. The Elves dutifully offered the equipment out to their masters.

"I am yours to command," said Cearanth, stating the obvious.

"Allow me to explain things to Cearanth while we are prepared," said Agranth to the king who approached him with an armful of leather and trailing straps.

"Capital idea," said the King then set to work, his wife already starting on Cearanth. Both dragons stood still as they were being saddled up, the true skill in saddling being in the correct tensioning of the straps to ensure a secure mount yet enabling free breathing and wing work. Both the King and Queen were experts in this field.

In clipped sentences Agranth told all he knew of his adventure and even Cearanth, lady that she was, had difficulty in stopping her jaw from sagging. It was incredible.

"Incredible, isn't it?" asked the King as if he had heard her thought, and stepped back to admire his handiwork. The Queen nodded too although she took as much pleasure for her husband's excitement at an adventure as she did her own.

"Indeed, your Majesty," agreed Cearanth.

"And you get to play as well," said Agranth rather magnanimously. Before she could answer the Queen interrupted.

"Now, no squabbles," she chided. "We are all in this together. Ready my love?" she called across to her husband.

"With you, my sweet, always," he beamed back.

The two dragons needed no second bidding and laid flat on the floor to allow their charges to mount. They waited patiently while their Royal Highnesses strapped themselves in then turned together towards the gaping portal and the open sky beyond.

Agranth brought his head close to Cearanth's.

"Ready for a real adventure?" he asked quietly.

"Always." Cearanth smiled at him.

"Me too." Agranth smiled back then he lifted his head high. The glint of excitement in his eye matched that of the Elf King on his back.

"On!" he said loudly. "To Unicorn Glade!" And launched straight into the blue, Cearanth and the Queen only a single wing beat behind him.

* * * * *

Word had somehow got about.

Blairoggin could only guess at how. Perhaps from the cloud-hoppers or moongliders, or maybe the obvious increase in activity in and around Unicorn Glade was enough to spark interest and rumour. Whatever, the word had most definitely got about.

While Naiouli and Oaken-Pel had retired to the mystic woman's castle to discuss whatever it is those magic types discussed, Alcor had found himself a nice sleeping tree and Kizzy had settled contentedly beneath it. Joining them in the age old waiting game the Keeper of the Keys found himself a nice spot of dark shade just inside the woodland edge and also settled down in a loose coil. It was a while later, when the cool shadow had almost lulled him into a light doze, that he first felt a sense of activity within the woods. A moment later he became aware of movement around him in the forest. Remaining motionless he used his excellent low light vision to good effect and soon spotted those who stealthily approached. With that feeling of inner glee that comes when seeing while being unseen, he began watching those who hoped to be watchers themselves.

There were of course already eyes on the lookout. Within the Glade itself stood Crystal with an accompanying herd of lesser Unicorns surrounding her, eyes and ears alert for possible danger. But they could not see what Blairoggin now saw. The odd flash of colour flitting through beams of sunlight that lanced down to splash upon the forest floor. He watched closely, but it was only when one of the mysterious, almost insect sized flying objects settled on a low plant stem nearby did he actually see what they were. He allowed himself a smile.

No longer than the breadth of the end of his snout, one of his very, very distant cousins flitted down and landed delicately on a broad petalled bloom in front of him at the very edge of the Glade. Without moving a muscle he examined the tiny flower dragon intently, finding himself looking at an exact, exquisite miniature of a full sized dragon apart from their remarkable chameleon properties. As he watched the tiny creature flicked out its long thin tongue into the heart of the bloom, drank in the droplets of nectar then changed before the huge dragon's crystalline eyes to become the same colour as the flower itself. A little Elysian wonder and Blairoggin enjoyed a pleasant time watching enraptured as the flower dragons, in ones and twos, zipped about around the edge of the Glade sipping from the coloured cups of the forest flowers. Every once in a while the little living gems would stop, cock one beady eye towards the centre of the Glade to check that they had not missed anything, then resume their nectar gathering.

Then a second, different type of movement caught his eye. Clusters of flashes of silver came swooping through the forest, darting between the trunks before disappearing in an instant as they landed somewhere out of sight. Picking up the many toned humming sound of their wings before hearing the misty sounding, unintelligible chatter of lots of quiet, secretive voices all speaking as one, Blairoggin raised an eye ridge in surprise. Now there was something you didn't see every day. At least not in large numbers.

A cluster of these shiny winged ones quickly spotted the great dragon, their low light vision at last as good as his Blairoggin decided, and after buzzing about at a safe distance for a while one of them got up the nerve to approach. Their apparent leader landed lightly on a long bough near his head. Glitters of darting silver flashed and within seconds a long row of winged people stood watching him keenly.

At first glance they looked just how one would imagine faeries to look. Only a couple of feet tall with little pointy toed boots woven from the softest moss, silkworm tights or breeks and shirts all in soft woodland colours and with hats of acorn cups or bell flower blooms.

They all had cherubic faces and their wings melted into blurs when they flew and twitched too and fro like butterflies when they were stationary, the fine gossamer membranes shimmering like moonbeams. But these weren't ordinary faeries.

These were faeries of the wildwoods. Usually they were very elusive although few people actually went out of their way to look for them. Any Elves who travelled deep into the Elysian forests were wary of them, and for good reason. The idyllic picture of charming woodland folk now forming before Blairoggin was soured slightly by the sight of the miniature swords at their belts and the tiny crossbows and quivers of bolts slung across their chests.

If the faeries of the wildwoods had also come to watch, he thought, then they must be expecting something quite out of the ordinary.

"Are you part of the coming gathering?" asked a squeaky, high pitched voice suddenly.

Blairoggin had to remember to keep his voice low. The wildwood faeries had very sensitive hearing and he didn't want to hurt or frighten them.

"What gathering?" he whispered politely.

"Haven't you heard? There's to be a great gathering here. Unicorns, wizards, moongliders.... and dragons," the lead faerie added as an afterthought.

"Oh, that gathering." Blairoggin nodded slowly. "Yes, I suppose I am part of the gathering then." He tried to make it sound as if it were something that happened to him every day.

"Good," came the same squeaky voice. "Well, we've come along to watch. Don't mind us though, we won't hurt you."

At that Blairoggin roared with laughter. He'd only closed his eyes momentarily as he exploded with mirth but when he looked again there wasn't a faerie in sight. At the unexpected noise all the little flower dragons too had vanished in their own way, freezing motionless wherever they were and instantly assuming the same colour as their immediate surroundings. The forest surrounding Unicorn Glade, only an instant before a hive of activity, was suddenly still and apparently devoid of life.

"Oops. Sorry," said Blairoggin sheepishly and settled back down in his coil to await the return to activity of the gathering watchers.

He didn't have to wait too long, but the activity wasn't exactly what he was expecting. With eyes peeled and scanning the forest floor it was with some surprise that he saw a shadow cross it, cast from above.

Looking up he saw a dragon circle the Glade, recognising the flyer instantly as Decorum. Ignoring the forest dwellers who miraculously reappeared on the instant, all eyes looking skyward, Blairoggin moved out of the shade of the trees. As if his appearance into the sunshine were some kind of signal the circling Gate Keeper swept lower and came in for a landing.

Barely had he touched the green earth when the unknown Elf sitting on his back made it plain with much waving of his arms that he wished to dismount. Clearly this passenger had failed to impress Decorum, Blairoggin decided, for his fellow dragon all but shucked the Elf off with a shrug of the shoulder making him stumble to the ground in an untidy heap. A travelling bag landed beside him with a thump. It was only when the Elf had regained his feet and began aggressively straightening his clothing that Blairoggin, who was already moving forward to greet the unusual pair, recognised the Elf as a wizard.

"Thank you *very* much," the wizard was saying, his voice acidic with sarcasm as he eyed up the great beast and flicked pieces of grass from his sleeve.

"Pleasure," replied Decorum in an off hand way but followed it up with a menacing, fang filled grin. For added emphasis he slowly licked his lips. Tourmalane nervously turned away, no longer wanting to look the dragon in the eye.

"Er... yes... well. What happens now? Oh!" he gasped as he suddenly found another huge dragon standing behind him.

"Naiouli will no doubt be out in a moment to explain things to you, along with Oaken-Pel," said Blairoggin courteously. "Blairoggin by the way. Keeper of the Keys, at your service."

Tourmalane rudely ignored the introduction.

"Naiouli and Oaken-Pel? I say... ah, yes. Look, there they are now." The wizard pointed dramatically to where the pair stood outside the castle gate and before either dragon could utter another word strode purposefully off towards them, and more importantly for him, away from the menacing dragons.

"Well, what a nice Elf," said Blairoggin curtly, not often a user of sarcasm himself, but carrying it off well enough.

"Just a bit pompous," said Decorum dismissively. "But he soon knew just whose back he was riding on though."

"Ah," said Blairoggin knowingly and nodded sagely, which Decorum seemed to like.

"So tell me then, oh Keeper of the Keys," the Gate Keeper smiled, briefly basking in what he thought was unspoken praise. "What's going on then?"

Blairoggin shrugged and looked on as the wizards greeted each other on the other side of the Glade.

"I'm not really sure, but I can tell you this much. Whatever it is, it's all go, my friend. Naiouli now has two of the three wizards with her. Bizarh has gone off to who knows where and Agranth has flown back to Talla-Weyre to see the King himself."

"The King's dragon was here?" asked Decorum incredulously.

"Yes. And I'll tell you something else. Apart from Kizzy and Alcor who are asleep by that tree, everybody else here is wide awake and waiting to see what will happen next. All I know for sure is that Bizarh has really stirred something up."

"Yeah?"

"Yes. D'you know, there are even wildwood faeries among the trees along with flower dragons and those Unicorns." Blairoggin nodded to where Crystal and her herd stood patiently. "All of them watching and waiting. Who knows what will happen next."

It was the biggest speech Decorum had ever heard Blairoggin make and he stared in amazement at the dark blue dragon. It was a few moments before he could gather his own thoughts.

"Yes... well, don't look at me." He shrugged and felt his own little passengers, who although fatigued were still listening intently, move on his back. "Look, let me put Zoozie and Sirus into that sleeping tree with their own. Poor things, they're tired out. Then you can tell me just how the King's dragon is involved in all this... this... whatever it is."

With that the dragons of stature moved to the tree line, and once Zoozie and Sirus were comfortably settled alongside their friends, the two great beasts also settled, close together under the trees in loose coils. They talked together in low voices, rejoining the steadily growing throng of watchers in and around Unicorn Glade.

Because there was yet more to see.

Later in the day, as the sun began to creep closer to the horizon tree tops, a flurry of activity from the wildwood faeries, who had stationed themselves high up in the canopy as self appointed lookouts, announced the approach of another arrival. The whisper came down.

Another dragon.

This time, as well as Blairoggin and Decorum, Naiouli, Oaken-Pel and Tourmalane walked out into the Glade to meet the approaching flyer, ready to greet him when he landed.

It was Blairoggin who first recognised the flying style and colour.

"Bizarh!" he gasped. "By the twin moons! When we all set off didn't he go in the completely opposite direction to Unicorn Glade? He must have flown like the wind to get back here so soon."

"That's all very well," said Decorum impatiently. "But who's that he's got tucked beneath him? That's not how a dragon carries an Elf. Surely that can't be the third wizard?"

It was impossible to identify the Elf in his unusual travelling position as Bizarh approached, clasped as he was in the dragon's paws. The forest dragon was his normal green self and Binnie was as ever there on his back along with the sleeping Mira, but it was only as he swept low and came into land that he released the Elf, in that moment of stillness as he stalled just above the rich grass. The black clad figure had to move fast. A scant moment after he'd hit the ground Bizarh executed one of his usual crash landings and the wizard had to run for his life out from under the green beast to avoid being crushed beneath the dragon's rapidly descending body.

Even as the wizard pulled to a stop and turned to glare angrily up at Bizarh there were gasps of recognition from around the Glade.

The Unicorn herd gathered quickly and protectively in front of Crystal. In the blink of an eye all the flower dragons disappeared into the colours of the plants they were on. Some of the wildwood faeries threw down their weapons and shot straight off into the forest without looking back, while the braver ones flashed out of sight, hiding in the nearest hole, bush or tree they could find. The two castle dragons simply looked on in stunned silence, as did the two other wizards. It was Naiouli, her mindword popping suddenly into everyone's head as if she had momentarily lost her mental control and blurted it out, that announced their latest arrival.

Goth!

To everyone's amazement the dark wizard, feeling the fear emanating from everyone around him and seeming to momentarily bathe in it, bowed deeply to his welcoming committee. A nasty, self satisfied grin appeared on his hairless face.

"At your service, Naiouli," he said brightly, not a word of truth in the sentence. "With Oaken-Pel and Tourmalane too I see. What pray does it all mean I wonder?"

Naiouli was saved any reply to the sarcastically delivered question by a sudden whooshing overhead as a double shadow slashed across the Glade.

Everyone looked up, amazed that this extraordinary day could supply any more astounding surprises. But this one topped even the sudden arrival of the Dark One for jaw-dropping effect.

"Agranth, Cearanth *and* their Royal Majesties!" whispered Decorum in awe. "This whole thing gets more unbelievable by the minute!"

The royal dragons produced effortlessly perfect landings and settled with barely a tremor onto the soft grass before the watching throng. Agranth and Cearanth dipped low and, after unstrapping, their Majesties dismounted and approached, the dragons a few paces behind.

Without a word everyone bowed deeply, although one not as deeply as the others noted Bizarh, glancing sideways at Goth.

"Rise, my subjects," said the King rather magnanimously, yet still managing not to sound patronising. "We are only here to offer what help we can, and of course my dragons are at your disposal Naiouli." He smiled at the mystic and offered out a hand. Everyone there bar the Queen and Naiouli herself showed surprise that His Royal Highness should even know her. Ignoring the looks she gently took his hand and pressed the back of it to her forehead. Whatever words passed between the two went unheard by everyone else, but as she finished and drew away the King's smile broadened considerably. The Queen stepped up and stood close beside her husband. She smiled at everyone, but the gesture did not go unnoticed by Cearanth, the first time the Queen's dragon had ever seen her Majesty display anything even remotely near jealousy regarding her husband's feelings towards any of his subjects.

"Tell me, Naiouli," she said, still smiling. "What is to be done now? Agranth has told us what he can about the creeping brownness that threatens Elysia and that you have set these good dragons to work to gather up the wizards needed. It appears that everyone is here, yet does not appear to know what follows."

Your Highness. The respect in Naiouli's mindwords was clear. *Forgive me. The wizards here are essential to repairing the damage already done. As it is their magic and auras that are entwined within the brownness spell, it is these same auras that are needed to help undo it.*

"So it can be undone?"

Yes, but preparations must first be made. Oaken-Pel will explain further while Tourmalane and Goth assist me with this work.

The mountain wizard, eager to help in anything that had close involvement with the King, stepped forward first.

"Tourmalane." He introduced himself. "I am at your disposal your Highness, ready and willing to do anything you wish."

Makes a change, thought Decorum sourly, but said nothing.

"Thank you," said the King then turned expectantly to the third wizard.

Goth however simply crossed his arms over his barrel chest. He did not wish to show open disrespect to the ruler of Elysia but had no desire to join in with this sickening display of royal fawning. Especially after he had been brought to Unicorn Glade against his will.

"Your pardon your Majesty." His voice was smooth, soft and oily. "But I do not think that I am involved with this, this creeping brownness." The tirade of hard looks shot at him from the others bothered him not a jot. "So I do not see why I should participate in these rites."

There was a short silence before Agranth, towering up and over his master, looked coolly down on the bare-faced Elf and said quite calmly.

"Perhaps those who would help in this work might be looked on favourably by His Majesty at some later date. Especially when the time comes to review the recent use by some of certain, unauthorised spells?"

Most of those gathered looked puzzled by the unexpected remark, except Naiouli, who allowed a small smile to tug at the corner of her mouth.

Goth, the memory of his unexplainably lost and highly illegal death spell springing to the forefront of his mind, took only a moment to reconsider. He bowed to the King.

"But of course, if the King wills it, I am his to command."

"Excellent!" The King beamed, his jolly demeanour not wavering in the slightest. Those few dragons in the know wondered if the Royal Elf was aware of the veiled threat, but the King was an Elf of depth. Who knew exactly what he knew? Few were privy to his deep thoughts and so, as to any further developments he might take on this subject, only time would tell.

Oaken-Pel stepped forward, stopping further speculation.

"My liege," he said warmly.

"Oaken-Pel." The King nodded and both Royals smiled. "We have heard much of your good works. It is an honour to finally meet you."

"The honour is mine," came the heartfelt reply. "And with your permission, I would explain what is intended to stop the further advance of the creeping brownness."

"Please." The Royal couple nodded together.

The wizard nodded in return, moved to the centre of the gathering and smiled broadly as all eyes fell on him, it clear that he was beginning to enjoy being the centre of attention. Dramatically he waved one arm.

"This, your Majesties, is Bizarh."

"Ah, the forest dragon," said the King enthusiastically and quickly ran his expert eye over the huge green beast. "My, but you are indeed a fine fellow. And a free dragon too. No master?"

"N... no... er...your Kingness." Bizarh stammered, never before having met a very important person. He had no clue as to what was supposed to happen next.

"Splendid!" The King clapped his hands with glee, apparently unconcerned with Bizarh's uncertainty.

"And so rare," said the Queen to no one in particular, joining in with her husband's admiration. "I hope you will allow us both to join in your grand adventure?" She shot a dazzling smile up at him and Bizarh's heart leapt.

"No problem... er... yes... ah, it would be my honour." He finally remembered how all the others had spoken to their Highnesses.

"Bravo!" acknowledged the King.

Agranth smiled, wondering if the King would ever run out of excited expletives. Cearanth meanwhile looked Bizarh over with a casual, but quietly admiring eye, as Blairoggin and Decorum grinned to see their green friend as captivated as they were the first time they'd been exposed to the personal and physical beauty of the Queen.

"Well..." said Oaken-Pel, wanting to add 'when you've quite finished' but prudently not doing so. "He was the dragon that started everything going after the discovery of the creeping brownness. But now it is our task to stop it. To this end Naiouli has gathered the wizards necessary to combine in its defeat. What must be done to achieve this is to create a transmission conductor. A conduit for carrying the rectifying spell into the brownness at its point of origin."

"Huh?" said several voices together." Goth just scoffed, no one knew whether it was at the ignorance or the explanation. Oaken-Pel smiled thinly.

"What I mean is a rod. A staff or some such, stuck into the soil where the brownness started. We wizards will send magic down it to put things right."

"Well why didn't he say so in the first place?" asked Decorum gruffly to Blairoggin. The Keeper of the Keys just shrugged.

"And how is this done?" asked the King.

"The three wizards will combine three spells in the first instance to create the rod."

"But isn't combining spells by different wizards rather dangerous?" asked the Queen quietly.

Oaken-Pel smiled, both at the Queen's apparent knowledge of the ways of magic and to calm her fears.

"Not dangerous, your Highness, just a little unpredictable. The problem is that when spells are combined from different sources it is impossible to judge the exact amount of input from each of those sources. Thus the final product of such combination spells will always do the task it was created for, but doesn't always take on the exact form or shape originally planned."

"So it reflects in some way a part of each of the original spell casters?"

"Well done!" Oaken-Pel exclaimed to the Queen before he could stop himself. "Pardon me, your Highness, but that is it exactly." He was truly impressed with her deduction. There were not all that many outside the world of wizardry that even remotely grasped the complexities of spell creation and casting.

"I hope you are taking note, Goth," said Agranth quietly but clearly, echoing the sudden thought of those around him. After all, the Dark One's reputation was well enough known, even by those who had never seen him before.

For a moment Goth never answered or even acknowledged the barbed comment. He had been in deep thought. A plan had formed inside his twisted mind. A great plan. And like all great ideas it had come to him in a sudden flash of devious inspiration. He suddenly saw a golden opportunity. A way to attain all that he craved, all the more satisfying in its attainment because it would be realised by deft and skilful deception. If events could be manipulated to his will. Which was his forte. All those around him could not know that danger was suddenly present in Unicorn Glade.

"Of course I will give the scheme my full support," he said smoothly. "If my aura and magic are needed to end this strife and hazard to our homeland then I am glad to give it." The dragons narrowed their eyes in suspicion at such a change of tune. Goth ignored them. "Let us wizards combine our strengths to create the necessary tool and then we can *all* go to the source of this creeping brownness and witness its destruction."

Involvement with destruction sounded more like the infamous Goth and this drew cautious nods of agreement from the others.

"Capital!" exclaimed the King once more. "I think I would very much like to see some splendid spell work in action, wouldn't you, my sweet?"

"If you think so," the Queen agreed, and was at once slightly unnerved by the sudden grin that appeared on Goth's face.

"Then it is all agreed," said Oaken-Pel cheerily, who turned to face the castle at the edge of the Glade. "Let us away to Tourmalane and Naiouli to begin preparations to make the rod."

Goth nodded, bowed deeply to the King and Queen then led off towards Naiouli's home. Oaken-Pel fell in behind him so, with everyone now at his back, no one could see that nasty, satisfied grin that had reappeared on Goth's face.

The first part of his plan was already in place.

The oldest, wisest, and all seeing Unicorn, Crystal.

8
Forging A Great Power

Dusk had fallen and all those who waited in Unicorn Glade came alert as the three wizards and Naiouli emerged from her castle and made their way to the centre of the glade. Everyone else gathered about the small group in a large semi-circle, giving them room to move while wondering just what would happen next.

The first thing Naiouli did, as she had done once before, was to call softly out into the night the name that no one knew. And once again, after she had called three times, the air began to fill with a soft buzz and a few moments later everyone was lit up with the eerie glimmer from the light of thousands of glowbugs. The little creatures had once again chosen the high ground to give maximum illumination and so all the dragons' heads and necks, which towered above those gathered, were festooned with the little living lights. Everyone looked around at everyone else, unable to stop themselves from grinning at the sudden display.

The King and Queen were quite naturally at the head of the gathered watchers. Fanning out around them was the largest number of Elysian dragons of stature gathered together in many, many years. Agranth and Cearanth stood, as was always their place, behind their masters. To the right of them was Decorum with Zoozie and Sirus perched attentively on one shoulder. Next to him was Blairoggin, Alcor and Kizzy having assumed their usual places high up on the dragons' brow. The Queen shot him a glance and a smile. This time the Keeper of the Keys didn't mind in the least if he looked silly. Not if it won him even a brief smile from her Royal Highness. To the left of the Royal dragons stood Bizarh, Mira and Binnie proudly taking a shoulder each, honoured to be associated with the dragon that the King and Queen of Elysia were so impressed with.

To Bizarh's left was Crystal, silent and majestic as ever, with her entourage of lesser Unicorns around her. They too watched in silence, apparently totally unconcerned by the constant to-ing and fro-ing of the wildwood faeries that flitted about and around them. Mind you, it didn't take long to realise that the little people never flew far from the herd, using their group almost as cover, or protection, the best to be had within the open glade. The Unicorns didn't seem to mind either the large numbers of little flower dragons that clung lightly to their hides. Weighing next to nothing and as white in colour as the hair they perched on, it needed a keen eye even to spot their presence. Blairoggin's excellent night vision allowed him this view and he smiled to see his little country cousins so close yet unobserved by those around them.

Naiouli stepped forward, bowed deeply to everyone then began to explain what was about to happen. Mindwords created no need to shout and everyone listened intently to the words inside their heads.

We must build the transmission rod needed to act against the tri-spell of the creeping brownness. But it cannot be simply made with sweat and toil. It must both carry and fight powerful magic, so it too must be made with magic.

As you have all in some way or other been involved with this battle against the brownness, it seems only right that you should witness the creation of the weapon to be wielded against your enemy.

Many eyebrows and ridges went up at this. All Elysia knew that magic, real, working, serious magic, was always done behind closed doors. The spectators eyed the wizards behind Naiouli with renewed interest. All there including Goth were bright eyed with keen intent. Clearly they were all eager and pleased to be a part of a rare event within the magical world. But they were not aware of this sudden scrutiny, all three huddled together with Oaken-Pel at their centre, as one consulting the big leather bound book open in the wizards' hands. After a final agreeing nod they stood straight and Oaken-Pel slammed the book shut with a loud clap. Tourmalane stepped forward and held out his travelling bag to Naiouli, the top gaping open.

The mystic woman reached in and produced from its mysterious depths a dark looking length of... something. A grey, almost oily looking cylinder only as thick as her wrist and about as long as her elegantly slender forearm. The cylinder seemed solid enough but its surface didn't appear to stay still. Almost as if it were squirming to break free of her grip even though, on closer inspection, the, whatever it was, wasn't actually moving.

Naiouli held the cylinder out before her so that everyone could have a good look.

This, is a piece of carbonium, she explained. *It is magicked matter. Not many have seen it like this, in its raw state.* She smiled at the looks of amazement on the others' faces, staring as they were, almost transfixed by the still, yet somehow moving mass in her delicate fist. *It is not inert and dead like stone, nor is it alive like the birds in the trees. It is somewhere in between.*

"Always carry a bit with me when I travel," interrupted Tourmalane rather smugly.

Very fortunate for us, Naiouli continued. *Carbonium is extremely useful for it can be moulded by magic. And that is what we shall do here now. We,* she indicated to her wizard companions, *will need to combine several spells to accomplish this and each must play their part.*

There were a few knowing nods from those who listened. No wonder the three wizards looked excited. A combination of two spells was unusual enough. More than that was enough to get even the most laid back wizards' undivided attention.

Oaken-Pel will cast an energy spell into the carbonium. This will create the power needed to enable the bar to change.

Tourmalane will throw a construction spell, it is after all his carbonium. She smiled but no one else did. *This will move the near living, energised material and make it develop and bond into its new type of matter.*

Goth will simultaneously throw a shaping spell, putting the new matter into its revised form and cause it to solidify there.

I will call up the elements spell. The mindwords somehow

impressed the extra importance of this particular spell on those around her and the watching wizards nodded, as if appreciation of her use of this spell. *This will create and store up vast amounts of energy and all the conversion magic within each of the others' spell auras, and hold it within the rod, ready to be released at the right time into the brownness.*

Now, we all know that there are four elements. I will call up those of Earth, Air and Water. All found in the ground where our conversion magic will do its work. The fourth element is of course Fire. This final piece of the spell will be the trigger which releases the powerful spell into the ground. And that is where you come in, my fine dragons.

The five great beasts jerked to sitting attention at that.

"Us?" they said almost as one.

Yes. You all are capable of being the trigger. It would be too dangerous for any normal fire to set off a thing of such power, so dragon fire it must be. And with so many different aspects of wizardry acting both together and against each other within this complex magic tool, it is impossible to say just how much dragon fire will be needed to release the spell. The energy within the rod will be wound so tightly that a single puff from one dragon may be enough. But then again it may take several of you working together to achieve that same aim, who knows with so many variables at work in one place?

It was the first time anyone had ever heard Naiouli state an uncertainty. Perhaps that was the moment when those in Unicorn Glade truly realised the dangerous nature of what they were about to attempt.

But do not forget, she continued as if she had said nothing particularly untoward, *once the transfer rod has been created there will be several combined spells and three of the four elements bound up in combination within that rod. It will from that moment on be an instrument of great power. Power for the potential of great good but also of great destruction. It must be respected. Such a thing could cause terrible catastrophes if it fell into the possession of the wrong or untrained hands.*

The gravity of her warning was not lost on anyone and they all nodded solemnly, even the little flower dragons.

Good. Naiouli allowed another small grin to flit across her face. *Stand back then, and we will begin.*

All the watchers retreated a few steps and spread out into a wide semi-circle.

When Naiouli considered them to be at a safe distance she mouthed a few silent phrases, the only time her soft lips were actually seen to form the shape of words, then gently released the carbonium bar. To everyone's surprise it did not drop immediately to the ground, but hung unnaturally in the night air a few feet above the soft earth, all the time its strange surface continuing to swirl.

Then the three wizards moved into position so that they were surrounding the bar while holding an equal distance from both it and each other. The other two magical Elves' eyes settled on Oaken-Pel.

The woodland wizard drew himself slowly up, summoning his aura from within, and thrust his arms out at the carbonium. With unworldly, unintelligible words spilling in an almost constant stream from his mouth and brow furrowed in concentration, his glittering eyes bored hard into the swirling surface of the bar. Everyone suddenly felt the air about them come to life, crackling with ionisation. Oaken-Pel was summoning up energy. Waves that rippled the air swam out in a stream from his open palms, crossing the distance between them and the bar. Simultaneously the little moongliders gasped.

"I see his aura," whispered Mira to Bizarh. "It is very, very strong."

Unheeding, Oaken-Pel's open palms snatched into fists and the wavering air enveloped the carbonium. At once the encapsulated air immediately surrounding the bar flared into light, a sudden, great lantern of light that lit up all the watchers and a large proportion of Unicorn Glade. Sweat was now beading on Oaken-Pel's forehead and with a great effort he shouted a tongue twisting spellword and smashed his fists together. Small, but eye-flinchingly blue bolts of lightning crackled within the wavering sphere, each bolt stabbing into the bar of carbonium. The swirls seemed to flinch with each strike. Oaken-Pel stepped back then with a great, satisfied sigh as the lightning bolts pummelled the bar with increasing ferocity.

For a few moments more everyone watched in stunned silence as the punishment continued. Then they all saw a change, noticing the light suddenly beginning to dim and the bolts slackening in frequency. For now the carbonium, rather than being hit by the electrical charges was actually absorbing them, sucking them up the instant they appeared. Within a few seconds the ball of light surrounding the bar was all but gone, the bar had sucked all the life out of it. And as the white light went, it was replaced by a soft blue glow coming from within the bar, itself now also a soft blue colour. It had its own illumination, emanating from the power within, the brightness of the glow subtly changing with the swirl of the almost living surface.

Tourmalane and Goth nodded in satisfaction. Oaken-Pel nodded briefly back in acknowledgement and stepped right back to let his fellow wizards play their own part.

The mountain wizard and the Dark One both drew themselves up to full height and began their own chants. Sung together, Tourmalane's was high and softly melodic, the unrecognisable syllables swooping up and down with mysterious inflections on certain words. Goth's in contrast was low, flat and almost monotone. Concentration now was total and together the words wove an almost unearthly, mysterious duet of incomprehensible, but undeniably powerful, harmony.

Tourmalane punched out at the blue carbonium with one fist, gripped some imaginary handle in the air before him and slowly turned it a half rotation as if he were turning something into something else, an object from one plane into another. The carbonium quivered briefly then slowly began to follow this rotation beginning to spin in the same direction. Almost leisurely to begin with, it quickly gathered pace and in a matter of moments was turning fiercely, fanning out its blue light over the watchers while whirring loudly in the night air.

Goth in the meantime had been rubbing his palms together and massaging the empty space between them, as if kneading some invisible clay, prior to moulding into shape and form. Satisfied that whatever he was working had reached the right consistency, he held the invisible material up to his forehead and muttered some strange, but obviously carefully chosen, wizard words. No one noticed the small but highly charged energy ball that darted from the cuff of his dark sleeve and vanished into his cupped hands. He drew back a clenched fist and shot a glance across at Tourmalane. The wizard nodded. The bar was spinning at the correct speed, his construction spell poised for completion.

Goth took a long step forward and hurled his fisted shaping spell at the whirling ball of blue light.

The moongliders gasped again then looked at one another in fear and uncertainty. Unseen by all but they, the aura that followed the thrown spell contained a particularly vicious looking streak of blackness.

But there was nothing to be done about it now. The spell was cast. They could only watch along with everyone else. Watch and see what emerged.

The Dark One's spell flew fast into the ball of blue light and everyone felt the pressure wave that rippled back from the impact. The ball of light flared with such radiance that those with good night vision had to momentarily shield their eyes. The bar now was just an object of intense light and, as everyone looked on, agog, this ball began to stretch, drawing slowly out into a long, thin line. Small crackles of lightning danced about it and as the harsh light began to dim a long narrow shape could just be seen within the brightness. A rod was beginning to form.

It was now that Naiouli stepped forward once more.

She raised an arm and the long, glowing shape rose up until it hung like a meteor in the sky higher than the heads of the watching dragons of stature. Jumbles of unknown and seemingly unconnected words poured into everyone's heads. They all knew they came from Naiouli but no one looked at her, unable to drag their gaze from the thin bar of light.

EARTH!

The word exploded loudly inside everyone and at the same moment a core of soil from the earth directly beneath the glowing bar tore out of the ground with a cruel rending sound, rose sharply up into the night sky and was sucked into the light, disappearing into the shining bar as if by, well, magic.

AIR!

A gust of wind whipped up from nowhere, swept through the glade, swirled about the shocked watchers then spiralled up into the sky, following the soil into the bar. As quickly as it had come, it was absorbed and gone. While this was happening a single brooding, dark cloud was forming directly above the bar of light, blocking out the stars there, its underside reflecting back some of the light beneath it.

WATER!

The rain cloud burst with a great clap of thunder and rain lashed down towards the ground and those standing below. But no one got wet. Not a single drop reached the ground as every single bead of moisture was sucked into the light. It was as if the bar had a great thirst and in moments had sucked dry the rain cloud. The few wisps of arid mist left began to drift forlornly away on the light breeze.

DRAGON FIRE!

To everyone's utter surprise nothing at all happened. The bar simply hung for a moment more before beginning to dim noticeably. As the light lessened it began to drift slowly down. Naiouli stepped clear and they all watched in absolute silence as the bar of light settled gently on the ground beside the new crater, not keeling over to lay flat but only touching down softly to balance upright and unsupported on its tip. The glow dimmed more and more, Unicorn Glade awash with the silence, no one daring to breathe as they waited to see what the diminishing light would reveal. Soon it was low enough for the glowbugs to re-illuminate and as the last of the wizard induced light faded everyone stared in amazement at what stood before them.

Balanced effortlessly and rather elegantly on its pointed tip, not even piercing the ground but barely touching it, was a sword.

A magnificent, beautiful, deadly looking sword.

The blade was a shining example of perfect symmetry from its needle point up to the swirling. shapely cross guard. On either face of the blade were etched strange, Elfin rhunic markings. Above the cross guard the grip was an elegant, tightly wound spiral of many thin twists of silvery metal. Closer inspection revealed the end of each of the dozen twists to be topped off with a miniature depiction of a dragon's head, each one a great work of art in its own right. But even this wonderful craftsmanship was secondary to the pommel that crowned the sword. This was in the shape of a perfectly detailed mail glove and clutched in its fist was a glassy orb not much bigger than a bird's egg. But within this orb was that same, familiar swirl of bluish light, hypnotic and constantly changing. Disturbingly, once in a while the light would dim slightly as a black swirl would pass over its face before disappearing back within the other colour of the orb.

"A sword!" gasped the Queen quietly.

Only Naiouli's eyes were not on the sword. She was looking across at Goth.

A sword?

Goth smiled disarmingly and shrugged. The gesture went unnoticed by the others, all watching as their King slowly approached the gleaming, magnificent blade.

"A sword," he repeated. "And clearly the only one of its kind."

Yes, your Majesty. Not just a sword. THE sword. The sword of Elysia.

"May I touch it?" he asked, the request for permission sounding rather odd coming from the ruler of the land.

Of course. It is harmless unless the power within it is released. There was a brief pause before she added, *well, almost harmless.*

The King tentatively touched the softy glowing orb of the pommel with the tip of one finger then, satisfied that it was safe, gripped the handle firmly and hefted the sword aloft.

"My goodness! It seems to weigh next to nothing."

Goth smiled and stepped forward.

"Try it your Majesty. Strike something with it."

The King frowned then looked about for something to cut at. There was nothing obvious immediately to hand, he even glanced briefly into the gaping hole at his feet before realising that the only thing near him was actually the ground he stood on. Swinging the blade in a wide arc he hacked down at the defenceless earth. To his utter surprise and shock he felt no noticeable resistance to the swing of the blade and he completed the arc with a sweeping follow through. He had applied almost no effort, but was appalled at the result it caused. The blade itself looked as pristine and untarnished as it had moments before yet the King found himself staring down at a great slashed cut deep into the ground, the turf and soil torn asunder by the blades passing.

"By the moons..."

"It will cut through anything," explained Tourmalane flatly. "With the energies, spells and elemental power within it, it could do nothing else."

"Yes." Goth's smile was never more unnerving, his smugness amplified by the secret knowledge that another, vital part of his scheme was now in place. "No stone nor steel, armour or magic can stop it. The one who holds the sword of Elysia can enter anywhere or escape from anywhere or defeat any opponent. And all that even before the elemental powers within it are released." There was great pride in his voice as he spoke. The admiration he felt for the potential for destruction in the weapon he had helped create was plain.

The shocking realisation of the immense power within the blade now clutched in the King's fist had many of the group gaping.

"Oh, my," whispered the Queen in breathless horror. "What have we created here tonight?"

"Something that will save Elysia, your majesty," said Agranth coldly.

"Yes. But at what cost to Elysia in the future?" she replied quietly.
No one had an answer to that.

* * * * *

The rest of the night was spent in, well, *rest*.

After the magic, excitement and wonder of the birth of the sword of Elysia everyone tried as best they could to get some sleep before the coming of day. Everyone that is apart from the moongliders, who flitted off on their usual night forays.

The King and Queen, along with the three wizards, were offered the hospitality of Naiouli's home while the dragons and the rest of the forest creatures remained in the open glade. No one felt the least bit put out at what at first glance seemed to be a rather uneven state of affairs. It was right and proper that the bi-peds needed shelter and beds whilst the others stayed out. For these were their natural places, each of the creatures comfortable enough in their home surroundings. The castle dragons didn't care in the least, glad of the extra freedom and space. Besides, for warmth they all carried their own internal heating systems. Bizarh didn't mind at all because it had always been this way for him and his little forest friends. They knew no better.

The fresh new morning found everyone in high spirits and ready for whatever the day might throw at them. The dragons had awoken first, but remained still and quiet until their little slumbering partners the cloud-hoppers, who were snuggled against their great bulks for the warmth there, also awoke. It was at this time the moongliders returned but they did their best to stay awake to be a part of whatever happened next. Soon everyone was gathered once more in the middle of Unicorn Glade. Their majesties still clad in their flying gear, the wizards in their cloaks and capes. Somehow all the clothing looked neat, clean and freshly laundered. Almost as if by magic.

It was Binnie, watching the whole proceedings intently, who suddenly voiced a concern as she watched their majesties checking the saddle straps of their steeds. She spied with fear the sword hanging loose at the King's belt, secured there by a stout leather strap wrapped around the sword's cross guard and through the belt. She spoke quickly to Bizarh.

"Isn't that a bit dangerous? I mean, if the sword can cut through anything, if it rubs against the King's leg or Agranth's side won't they be badly cut? Doesn't the King realise he is in danger?"

Before the green dragon could answer a soft chuckle tinkled bell-like in the cloud-hopper's head.

Do not worry, my little friend. The sword is more than just a blade. It is almost a sentient thing. It of course has no will of its own but senses the intentions of its user. When it is at rest, like now, the sword is in stasis.

"Huh? Isn't Stasis one of the south land Elfin villages?" asked a by now totally baffled Binnie.

An even heartier laugh echoed through their heads this time. Naiouli floated across to the where the cloud-hopper stood.

Stasis simply means that the blade is calm. Sleeping if you like. If it were active all the time it would be a menace to everyone and everything around it. It could not be safely carried. Just by trying to rest the sword on the ground, it would immediately sink into whatever it was resting on, right up to the hilt. And as you say, accidentally brushing it against a leg would effortlessly remove the leg from the person it would normally be attached to.

"Oh." Binnie sounded and looked sheepish, but Naiouli bent down and gently patted the forest dweller's head.

Well done for asking, little one. It is something that the wizards included when they created the sword, planned from the beginning. But not many would have even thought of it.

The sheepishness went as quickly as it had come, replaced with a proud grin. Bizarh dipped his head to be close to his little friend.

"Smartie pants," he whispered out of the corner of his mouth but followed the remark with a wink.

"Yes," said the King, surprising everyone by addressing the little cloud-hopper directly. "I took a little while to think of that one myself. But with this in-built stasis thing, I can have a magnificent scabbard made for the sword when we return to Talla-Weyre."

The Queen smiled at her husband and his brimming enthusiasm. It was just the sort of thing he greatly enjoyed and really rather excelled in.

"That's all very well, my love, but shouldn't we deal with the problem at hand first?"

"Quite right," he exclaimed, not in the least bit perturbed by the gentle rebuff from his wife. Clearly his enjoyment of this great adventure easily won out over any discomfort he might feel at such a small thing. "Make ready my magnificent dragons! It is time for the off!"

Spoken jovially enough, for everyone else present the instruction was a royal command and those gathered sprang into activity.

Their Majesties mounted their blood dragons.

The cloud-hoppers and moongliders quickly flew up onto their dragon friends' backs, where the little night dwellers almost immediately latched tightly on and fell fast asleep. Blairoggin waited patiently while Oaken-Pel mounted warily and Decorum dipped low to allow a now eager Tourmalane easy access. Goth climbed onto Bizarh's broad green back as if it were his natural birthright. Almost as naturally, Binnie and a sleepy Mira moved as far away from the dark wizard as they could and still be safe. Not that Goth paid them even a moment's attention.

Our very best wishes to you all, my friends. Naiouli's mindwords were clear, warm and heartfelt. *All success on your venture. Our thoughts are with you.*

Crystal bowed deeply to everyone and even the King nodded in return. Then it was time to leave.

Even the wildwood faeries waved the flight of dragons off as one after another the great beasts coiled and launched up into the clear blue morning sky. As the Unicorns, flower dragons, faeries and of course Naiouli turned their eyes to the heavens, the beautiful mystic shading her eyes against the brightness, who could deny that the unprecedented sight of five dragons of stature flying together was enough to take the breath away.

The great winged beasts drew together into a shallow vee formation with Agranth and the King at its head. Then the magnificent display did one full circuit above Unicorn Glade in a spectacular fly past before striking out towards the north east, towards the heart of the great forests of Elysia, and towards the site of the ever spreading brownness.

With the forest canopy fleeing by below them the winged troupe pondered in silence on the event yet to come as they flew on towards their date with drama. Many thoughts were on how effective the sword of Elysia might be and how quickly it would take for the affected area of forest to recover from the damaging blight of the spreading brownness. It was only the wizards Oaken-Pel and Tourmalane who seriously questioned the certainty of the untried instrument of power they had created, but wisely kept their doubts close and silent within themselves.

Goth's just as pensive features though did not betray the completely different thoughts that filled his dark mind. Thoughts that were at that moment as dark as his reputation. While those about him held concerns on the possible future of Elysia and the forests, the wizard was intent on fine honing the dastardly plan he had hatched the day before. Plotting still as to how to bring the scheme to its black hearted fruition. The more he considered it the more his optimism grew. So far things had gone smoothly along his deviously plotted course.

He found it hard to stop himself from rubbing his hands together in glee at what had so far unfolded and to what was yet to come, but he had learned long ago to mask his thoughts from the prying eyes and minds of those around who might seek to thwart him. After all, the great scheme was already in motion, things already transpiring as predicted.

He had already introduced a few little 'added extras' into the magnificent sword that hung at the King's waist and, equally as important, he had also skilfully persuaded the Royal couple to accompany them all to the site of the brownness. Or more exactly, coerced them both to the place where the sword would be activated. Then the fun would really start.

Goth managed not to nod in agreement with himself and pictured the forthcoming events in his head, wrapping his plan around what he saw happening in his mind's eye.

When the sword was finally activated as a transmission rod, transmit wouldn't be the only thing it did, and nothing could stop it. And 'it' would mean that all the elemental power within the rod would make the special spell he'd concealed inside the weapon immensely potent. The spell that was illegal and never to be used without express permission of the King himself.

The great irony of it all was that the spell would actually be directed at the King. And his lovely wife.

The kill spell.

In fact, Goth decided at that moment, it would suit his purpose even more admirably if they all died. He cast a quick glance about at those in flight around him. The more the merrier, he thought, and besides, great plans often called for great sacrifices. As long as they were made by someone else. Yes, the fewer remaining witnesses there were, the better it would be.

For Goth had his sights set on nothing less than the very throne of Elysia!

With his scheme already in motion, it could not but carry on through now to what he considered to be its natural conclusion, he reasoned.

Once the dragon fire had activated the sword of Elysia, his plan would be unstoppable. The kill spell hidden within the complex majikery that made the sword would spring to deadly life. Goth would make sure he had retreated out of its limited lethal range and watch in safety as those gathered about the sword were struck down, leaving the way clear for him to pick up the reigns of the then leaderless Kingdom.

It would be quite simple after that, and he couldn't help a smirk flashing briefly across his face then, once their Royal Highnesses and their followers were safely dead.

With a relatively simple piece of magic the dark wizard could transform his outer appearance to that of the King. The chameleon spell wouldn't last all that long he knew, but easily long enough for him to go to Talla-Weyre where he could then, posing as the grieving King, retreat into seclusion within the royal palace to 'mourn' the tragic death of her beloved Majesty.

It would be rather a nice touch, he thought, if he commanded everyone in the kingdom to wear black. It was after all his colour.

Unseen by an understandably and just as distressed populous, Goth could then rule for years without having to show his own face. Then, once the memory of the Elfin people began to fade and their attention was turned to other things, he could concoct a new scheme to legitimately claim power in his own image. He'd have years to dream something up to that end and besides, with the twin powers of magic and policy at his disposal, he could achieve anything. As ruler, everyone would be duty bound do his bidding while his enemies could not escape his wrath. Especially with the sword of Elysia in his hand.

It was a truly dastardly, devious and dreadfully evil plot. And Goth had never before been more in his true element. The urge to laugh out loud and punch the air at the terrible magnificence of his scheme was almost uncontrollable but the Dark One managed it.

Containing his warped glee behind a suitably sour expression he stared off into the far distance and the prospect of what lay ahead. Only the glitter in his evil eyes gave any indication of the terrible impending calamity that was about to befall Elysia.

9

By The Sword

And then they were there.

The awesome flight of dragons approached the rim of the expanse of brownness to a soft chorus of gasps from their passengers. For an expanse was indeed what it had now become. Although it wasn't possible to see with the naked eye the awful blemish on the face of the land actually expanding, it had during the many days since its birth spread steadily out across the forest to become a huge tract of barren, dead wasteland. As the flyers crossed above its boundary edge, the line between vibrant green and bleak brown only appeared to be a gently sweeping curve. Allowing for a spread that worked its way outwards in an even, continuous creep, the entire circle of brownness was now vast. Agranth, the one with the most methodical and analytical mind, calculated that at their present speed it would take several more long minutes to reach its centre. It truly shocked even him to realise that the great land of Elysia now carried upon it a cruel, lifeless scar it would take a good day's march to cross!

The sight of it made all the smaller forest creatures huddle together in the middle of their dragons' backs to find whatever protection they could. The King and Queen found themselves fighting to overcome a sudden urge to immediately go to each other and hold on tight. The great dragons gritted their teeth and grasped onto the thought that they had come to do battle with this terrible, growing canker. Both the forest and mountain wizards hung their heads in shame, now knowing the part their spells had played in the creation of such a disaster. The Dark One felt his chest swell.

They flew on to their destination, the centre of the brownness, which was easy enough to see. That place where the dead and decay had been longest.

From the spreading edge of the blight where the green forest could be seen newly wilted, the decay rapidly became more and more advanced as they moved inward. The rotting of the forest was somehow accelerated. From newly dead trees, back through fallen timber and crumbling, flaking hulks of logs, the decay increased until, near the centre there was just grey, wind blown ash like dust and bare, sterile earth. And right at the centre, a terrible bullseye in a huge, awful and lifeless target, the bare, burnt ground was black. Like the colour of evil.

The flight circled this desolate, scorched spot once then settled down at its rim. Even Bizarh's usual, almost crash landing of a touchdown made little sound. The heavy soil seemed to absorb sound, deadening it.

Goth jumped smartly down from the green dragon's back and strode across the black ground to stand over the single pock mark that signalled the exact centre of the spreading death. The place where the tri-spell had fallen. With arms akimbo he turned to face the others and found them staring on in silence. In his black robes it was as if he had sprouted from the very ground beneath his feet. As if he were a part of it and what it was.

He dismissed their goggling. He had his own agenda. Power and wealth awaited him. The wealth would be nice, he thought, but it was the great power that he craved.

"There is no time to stand about and admire the view." He smiled at his little joke, which strangely left all the others aghast. "There is work to be done and we cannot delay. If we stay here too long we too will start to be affected by the creeping death."

"Go... Goth is right." Stammered Oaken-Pel, the first to finally find his voice, shocked as he was at Goth's both blatantly apparent joy and his great insult to Their Majesties by addressing them as common underlings. "We must act quickly or we will put ourselves in danger."

"Right!" barked the King rather too loudly, trying to put on a brave face before his subjects, although it didn't fit all that well over his shocked features. But he must look to be in command. Everyone of course knew he wasn't, but respected him too much to say so. So no one was surprised or embarrassed when he immediately turned to Tourmalane.

"So... what do we do now then?"

"Your Majesty." The wizard bowed. "You need to take the sword of Elysia and plunge it into the heart of the brownness. Where the spells fell."

All eyes fell on the black pock mark behind Goth's feet. The Dark One stepped aside, bowed and made a great sweeping gesture with his arms.

"Your Majesty," he said rather majestically. Was there a hint of mockery there also?

The King looked to his wife, who patted him on the forearm and offered her husband one of her warm, charm-filled smiles. Grateful, he nodded then walked with unnervingly silent footfalls towards the small black hollow of the pock mark.

Goth fell back into line and with the others he retreated until all the watchers were well back, all fully engrossed in the actions of their monarch. So engrossed in fact that none were aware of the Dark One as he slipped out of view, silently continuing to retreat.

The King stared bleakly down at the hollow before him, imagining that he could somehow feel the presence of death and evil emanating from the hole. Perhaps it wasn't all imagination? At that the ruler of Elysia gave an involuntary shudder, gripped the handle of the sword at his waist and drew the blade. The instant he had touched the sword it became active and so cut effortlessly through the stout leather thong that held it to his side, the weapon hefting free without resistance.

Holding it briefly up in the air before him, the King drew a deep breath, inverted the blade and, grasping the hilt with both hands, plunged it straight down into the small black pit.

It cut deep and went smoothly down until the cross guard arrested its penetration. All the watchers felt a tremble in the ground around them and the King straightened, his features suddenly illuminated by the glow from the orb in the fisted pommel. A light not there a moment before. The ground shook once more and high in the air over the watching group, directly above the sword, small wisps of dark cloud began to appear, whipping tightly about overhead. The King beat a hasty retreat back to his companions and joined in the silent watch as the wisps rapidly became small, dark thunder clouds.

"The elements combine," said Oaken-Pel quietly.

"Then we need fire," said the Queen. "Dragon fire."

All eyes then turned to His Majesty. Whose own gaze turned naturally to Agranth. The King's dragon. The finest dragon in all of Elysia. It was a grand opportunity the great dragon of stature would once have taken without a second's pause. An honour his birthright and status dictated, with the permission of the King.

But Agranth had learnt much in a few short days. Learnt how those not of high office or birth could be as great as those who were. He gazed around at those beside him. The Keeper of the Keys and The Gate Keeper, both loyal subjects who risked the loss of all through desertion for a greater cause. The strange, unknown green forest dragon who had won Agranth's admiration for originally taking up the quest with no thought of redress or reward. Simply doing something because he knew it was right. Even the littlest forest dwellers, the cloud-hoppers and moongliders, had overcome their own fears, shyness and all the others' views of them as small and worthless, to become leaders of Elysia's great dragons of stature, pointing the way to the pivotal moment in time and place where they now all stood. The greatest dragon in the land had learned that honour and respect was not a birthright. It was a reward for one's actions in both thought and deed.

With a broad, fanged smile everyone at first assumed was one of self-satisfaction but was actually of self-discovery and enlightenment, the King's dragon turned to face Cearanth. She who was as loyal and true as he, but had always stoically played second fiddle to the great Agranth.

"I believe this honour is yours."

Cearanth's fanged jaw dropped quite unladylike open in shocked amazement.

The King gaped also for a moment before breaking into a huge grin. The Queen laughed out loud and clapped her hands together in glee, prompting all the other dragons, the little forest dwellers and both the forest and mountain wizards to grin widely too. None were fortunate enough to notice the absence of Goth or unfortunate enough to witness his altogether different grin as he strode purposely away behind them.

"Well?" prompted a hugely grinning Agranth as the Queen's dragon stood, dumbstruck.

"It... it... would, would be my honour," stammered Cearanth.

"Well, be quick about it then," chuckled Bizarh rather irreverently, eyeing the gathering storm clouds above them. "Otherwise we could all get wet if that little storm breaks."

Cearanth nodded a charming acknowledgement and glided smoothly over to the protruding sword hilt. It looked suddenly very small as she towered over it. Rising up to full height she drew in a deep breath.

With a sharp roar, crisp and loud in the oppressive silence, a bright tongue of flame lashed from her mouth, streaking downwards to engulf and incinerate the sword. But it never touched the glowing weapon. The flames seemed to concentrate sharply just above the bright orb of the hilt and swirled into a tight, narrow stream of hot light. As if they were being jammed into the neck of an invisible funnel immediately above sword hilt. Once concentrated into this tight needle lance of flame, the hot stream was sucked down and appeared to pierce into the top of the little glowing orb. In seconds all the light and heat had disappeared into it, absorbed, the only immediately apparent aftermath of this clash a sharp brightening of the light from the orb.

Cearanth stared down at the sword, momentarily breathless, then moved back to rejoin the others.

"What now?" she asked no one in particular, rather disappointed. She wasn't sure just what she had expected, but she'd certainly expected something more than that.

"Well..." Tourmalane had just began to shrug when the ground beneath them gave a great shudder. Everyone dropped into a sudden crouch to help retain their balance on the trembling soil, before movement drew them to look towards the sword hilt. It was slowly rising up!

The ground it was still embedded in was pushing up into a mound, lifting the sword hilt at its apex. In moments the hotly glowing ball of light in the mailed fist was at eye level. The light began to increase, soon bright enough to hurt and all the watchers began to back even further away.

Making them all flinch, a sudden clap of thunder rent the air overhead and a bolt of lightning stabbed down at the orb. At the same instant a similar lance of light grew out of the orb itself and the two met in the charged air just above the sword. The two shards of light became one and stretched into a single, arrow straight beam of power reaching from the sky to the earth. A deep rumble started far down inside the black ground, as if something living within it had been somehow cut by the magic sword and was now dying in agonising slow motion. The rumble spread out beneath them and moved rapidly off in all directions at once, Bizarh thinking the sound somewhat reminiscent of a disappearing heard of running Unicorns.

"It's working," whispered Oaken-Pel to Tourmalane, each wizard grinning at the other. Gasps from the others drew their attention back to the spectacle before them.

The beam of light was retracting from the clouds above, reducing in size till it settled as a short, stout pillar of light only a few feet high above the pommel of the sword. Both wizards frowned in puzzlement. This wasn't what was supposed to happen next.

A wisp of light separated from the pillar of power and swirled tightly around it, rapidly taking form into a small satellite.

It was at that moment that Bizarh and Binnie gasped in shock and horror of recognition. An electrical orb glowed into being before them. Just like the one Goth had launched at them, only this one looked an awful lot more powerful than the last. Bizarh looked about for the Dark One and at once saw him standing with arms folded across his chest, several hundred paces back. The arrogant stance he had also witnessed before made his heart sink in fear.

"Look out!" he cried in dreadful panic, turning back towards the bright light just in time to see the orb launch. Straight at the King!

No one heard Goth's distant cry of triumph as everybody froze in horror at the attacking lightening orb. Everybody but one. In response to Bizarh's warning cry Agranth just had enough time. Time enough to exert his great strength and reflexes as he leaned forward and flicked one wing around and in front of the King.

With a bright, arcing flash the orb struck the royal dragon's membranc. Agranth roared in pain and was flung back by the impact. The King was knocked from his feet by the blast and sprawled full length on the ground while the Queen, who immediately tried to rush to his aid, was prevented from doing so by Cearanth. The she dragon wrapped her wings about her charge and rolled to the ground and away to one side as a second orb flashed only inches wide and impacted with a sharp bang into the dark earth beyond them.

Pandemonium reigned as the sword of Elysia began spitting forth orb after deadly orb. They had no actual single target, the kill spell within the heart of the blade simply trying to eradicate everything within its range. The energy balls lashed out from the light beam every few seconds, as quickly as they could materialise from it. The King and Queen were being protected as best they could by their blood dragons who, by holding themselves between the pair and the orbs, were using their fast reflexes to dodge the attacks. Blairoggin and Decorum had both launched and, with neither Agranth or Cearanth able to do so without exposing their Majesties, were doing their best to draw some of the fire from the inexhaustible sword of power by swooping low across and around the sword. A very brave thing but soon one or other of them would miss-time their dangerous low level aerial jinks and be hit. The two wizards were simply hurling themselves out of harm's way as best they could each time an orb streaked towards them, banging into the ground close by and showering them both with clods of dead earth. But all knew they couldn't carry on their avoiding tactics much longer. They were already tiring. It was just a matter of time.

Bizarh also swooped, milling with the castle dragons. His first thought had been to get to Goth and force him to make the sword stop. But he knew by the time he had retrieved the Dark One and forced him to act it would all be over.

Binnie knew this too. She clambered precariously up onto the green dragon's shoulder.

"Hot, Bizarh! Think hot!" she shouted. "Your power can stop the orbs. I've seen it."

"What...?"

"Hot!" she cried even more urgently. "You can do it. Stop the sword."

Right. Hot, thought Bizarh and closed his eyes, trying hard to think hot thoughts. But nothing happened. He felt not even the merest flicker of warmth.

Then an orb came straight at him. It was almost upon them before he saw it, Binnie's shriek of fear making him flinch away at the very last second. A shriek that turned to one of pain as the orb flashed over Bizarh's neck, searing the scales there, and went so close to Binnie as to blast her from her perch. Bizarh was low at the time but the cloud-hopper still tumbled quite a way down onto the dark earth, thudding into the soft loam and laying very still.

The heat from the orb burn and the sudden hot fury within Bizarh at the sudden death of his friend was enough. More than enough. With a great roar he went uncontrollably into spasm. The forest dragon swelled. His wings grew and thickened, talons lengthened and his scales eclipsed to a deep bronze. Perhaps magical power knows magical power or that opposites attract, but as if his warping were some sort of signal or magnet to the energy bolts, as each one emerged from the sword's light beam they all swooped wildly through the air and zeroed in on the dragon. In reply he swooped right around the sword, above the heads of all those who cowered below, and drew all the airborne bolts away from his companions. The orbs hit the warp dragon's flanks with a great flash and fizz but he seemed to just shrug off the blows.

With a single, powerful flap of his wings he launched up over the sword hilt and somehow hovered stationary directly above it, poised in the dark sky between the light beam and the thunder cloud. Lit brightly from below, stark against the darkened backdrop on which he now threw a monstrous shadow, he was a great, fearsome apparition of menace and power.

Orb after orb spat from the top of the light beam straight up at Bizarh. In direct response he drew in a great breath. No one expected what happened next.

A gigantic tongue of bright green flame lashed down from the forest dragon's mouth. It swallowed up and snuffed out all the oncoming orbs and carried on down onto the light beam, which immediately turned bright green. The flames then struck the glowing, swirling orb of elemental power held in the mailed fist of the sword's pommel.

And like the dragon fire of Cearanth's before, the sword swallowed up the wondrous green flames. There was a sudden silence then, at a huge clap of thunder from the cloud above, the sword's swirling blue orb of power turned a luminescent green and the ground beneath them all shuddered anew.

The high mound of black soil immediately beneath the sword of Elysia seemed to somehow wriggle, as if attempting to shake off the shroud of the creeping brownness. Small green shoots suddenly pricked out from the black earth around the embedded blade. Like the expanding ripple on a pond where someone had tossed in a stone, green, new life sprang from the dark soil, moving steadily outwards from the point where the sword blade was buried. Out across the ground. Out past the King and Queen and the wizards. Out past Agranth and Cearanth. Past Blairoggin, Decorum, the moongliders and cloud-hoppers. And on out past Goth. The dead earth on which they had stood scant moments before was now a carpet of lush green shoots, some already becoming identifiable as the young growths of wild flowers.

The only one not to be totally amazed by this magical transformation was Goth. He roared in fury at his thwarted scheme, cursed the great warp dragon at the top of his lungs then turned and fled away across the new meadow. But he didn't get far.

With the anger still thundering hot in Bizarh's blood the forest dragon went straight after the black hearted wizard.

Everyone's jaw dropped in amazement as they saw Bizarh use his warp speed. He vectored in on the fleeing figure and, in the blink of an eye, flashed from above the sword to Goth, moving so quickly across the space between them that he was no more than a blur. At such a high approach speed the draught from his slipstream knocked the wizard down as he swept in and before Goth could fully find his feet Bizarh had crashed hard onto the green turf beside him and snatched the wizard up in one great claw. Without a single word Bizarh carefully eyed the ensnared elf with undisguised loathing and anger, then began to squeeze.

Goth gasped for breath, but to no avail. He could not even cry out. His eyes began to bulge and his tongue stuck grotesquely out from his head.

"Stop!" came a shouted command.

Inside Bizarh's fuddled, spasmed brain the shout somehow made itself heard, recognising it as a command issued by someone who was used to having his commands obeyed.

"Stop!" It came again and Bizarh reluctantly slackened his grip enough to allow Goth a breath, the wizard gratefully sucking in the precious air. Ignoring his captive's obvious relief, the warp dragon looked to where the shout had come from. He saw his Royal Highness the King striding purposefully towards him, followed closely behind by the Queen and all the other dragons.

Bizarh watched in silence as the King drew near, not once looking down at the wizard in his fist. The absolute disdain with which Goth was being treated totally unnerved him. Only a few moments before he had been seconds from death, but it was only now that he was truly frightened for the first time in his life. Absolutely terrified of not being noticed. Of being completely dismissed and ignored. He looked pleadingly at the King, who also ignored him as he stopped before Bizarh, looking sternly up at the great bronzed warp dragon.

The Queen watched in quiet admiration a few paces behind. All the others stared on in impressed amazement. They had never before seen His Royal Majesty so commanding, assertive, determined and, well, King like!

"Do not kill him, Bizarh," he said in a firm, steady tone.

"Why not?" demanded Bizarh, his voice deep, resonant and thick with anger. "He is a menace to all. He is ruthless, cruel and hateful. His actions have put you, the Queen, all of us and Elysia itself in great danger. And all for personal greed and power."

The King nodded. "I know this now."

"So why not kill him?" the warp dragon asked again. "You, we and all Elysia would be well rid of him. He deserves no better."

"True," agreed the King to everyone's surprise. "But you do."

"Huh?" Bizarh's single grunted surprise echoing what everyone else was thinking.

"If you kill him, my brave dragon, you bring yourself down to his level. If he dies now by your hand, in death he passes part of himself on to you. You become like him. A wise Elf once told me that you cannot kill a monster in cold blood without becoming a monster yourself."

The words stopped Bizarh cold. His brain was still befuddled by the warp power coursing through him, but whatever happened to his physical state during his transformation, it did not, could not alter his true being. The true person within himself. The good and honest person there. Deep down he already knew that the King was right. If he cold-bloodedly murdered Goth he would also kill his own goodness. He felt his fiery anger diminish. But still his warp side demanded retribution from the Dark One for his evil deeds.

"But what of revenge and repayment for all this devil has done?" Bizarh shook Goth out before everyone, the wizard's bald head lolling back and forth with the action.

"Leave him to me." The King's voice became softer, reassuring, confidence inspiring. "I will think of a suitable punishment. I will make sure he gets justice for his crimes. There are worse things than death, my wondrous dragon."

"But what sort of justice is there for what he has done? Killing off part of the Forests of Elysia. For the possibility of killing off all of Elysia. For trying to kill you, the Queen and all of us."

"But he did not succeed, thanks to you."

Bizarh ignored the great compliment. He just shook Goth one more time.

"And what about poor Binnie," wailed the warp dragon. "Is there justice for her?"

"Do not kill him for me," came a quiet, quivering voice from behind everybody else.

"Binnie!" exclaimed Bizarh joyously.

Everyone turned to look and saw the little cloud-hopper standing behind them, rather unsteady on her tiny hooves. She swayed slightly and looked more than a little dazed, but managed a small smile. Everyone, including their Royal Majesties, found themselves smiling back. Then they saw her injury. A broad, raw burn was striped across her back just behind the shoulders, a painful looking welt. But what they could not see hurt more. Small, heat cauterised stumps stuck sorely up from her back, all that remained of her membranous, glittering wings, instantaneously burned away by the passing of the energy bolt.

Behind them all came a soft whooshing sound, like a breeze passing through the drapes at an open window. When they all looked back Bizarh was his usual green self. His sorrow at the sight of his brave friend's injury, combined with the joy of seeing her alive had snatched away the last of his anger. In his normal state, as if only now aware of the weight in his paw, he looked finally down at Goth then eyed the King, more respectfully now. His Royal Highness simply nodded. Bizarh nodded in return, dropped the Dark One unceremoniously to the ground and lumbered over to Binnie.

The King pointed at Goth.

"Watch him," was all he said.

A command they were more than glad to obey, Blairoggin and Decorum moved immediately either side of the Dark One, towering menacing over him. As the King joined his wife and the others who were gathering happily around Binnie the heroine, Decorum dipped his head and said quietly.

"Me and Blairoggin aren't as nice as Bizarh. Just think about making any sort of false move and we will burn you to a crisp right where you stand, matey."

"Right," confirmed the Keeper of the Keys flatly, for once in total agreement with the Gate Keeper.

Goth saw their momentarily exchanged glances of mutual respect and felt their determination and hate towards him.

He humbly and very wisely did as he was told.

* * * * *

The magnificent flying wing of dragons of stature was once more airborne, retracing its path through the clear sky of Elysia towards Unicorn Glade.

Almost everyone was gazing down in admiration at the transformation of the previously barren and lifeless ground beneath them. Where once had been creeping death was now young, vibrant, new plant life. At best it had been hoped that the creation and application of the magical and powerful Sword of Elysia would merely stop the brownness and its inexorable spread. But used in combination with the astounding new found power of Bizarh the warp dragon, the brownness had been not only stopped, but dramatically reversed.

Although his green dragonfire could not reinstate the fallen trees or dead insect life, it could capitalise on the remains and use it as a readily available growing medium. Compost, the Queen had called it. Where there had been compost, which was of course everywhere within the brownness, new growth had sprouted the moment the mixed magic had reached it. A ripple of fresh greenery, spreading out from the sword's tip towards the very edge of the brown scar.

The magic had reached the edge before the flyers and as they passed over its bright new lushness many of them glanced admiringly back and forth from the scene below to the green dragon in their midst.

Bizarh seemed totally unaware of the attentions of his admirers. He was more intent on getting back to Unicorn Glade as quickly as possible to unload the unpleasant burden he carried.

Goth sat silent and passive in the centre of his broad back, although the wizard's eyes could not disguise the fury, hatred and contempt that burned there. Whatever punishment they dealt out to him, the dark wizard swore that they would all pay dearly for their mistreatment of him.

But he could do nothing now. On orders from the King the green dragon was under escort, flying below and ahead of the others with Blairoggin and Decorum on station on either side, just behind and above him. The castle dragons never took their crystalline gazes from the Dark One for a moment, silently willing him to do something stupid and give them the chance to end his menace once and for all. The cloud-hoppers and moongliders still rode on their backs as usual, Kizzy and Zoozie nosing into the slipstream while Alcor and Sirus slept in the bright sunshine, unperturbed at missing the glorious greenery below. Once past Bizarh's fine work and over the mature forest canopy they would not have been overly interested anyway. They lived there, saw it every day and hoped to return soon, once everything was finally sorted. They really had no more part to play in the string of events but His Majesty had said that as they had been an important part of the great adventure, it was only right and proper that they should see it through to the very end. He was truly a great and wise King, they had decided.

So too had Mira and poor, singed Binnie. Understandably unhappy at being parted from Bizarh but just as unwilling to travel with Goth, the King had offered them both a ride on his very own blood dragon. Agranth gave them both a wide, fang filled grin and said he would be honoured to carry them. And so the little forest dwellers, who had always felt they were of no importance, found themselves accompanying the King himself on his great, blood dragon, an honour that left them speechless. Although it still didn't stop Mira soon falling asleep to catch the sun's rays on her glittering wings. With no one to keep her company then, and unable to go to Agranth's shoulder to put her nose into the slipstream, Binnie decided to keep very quiet and sought out the place most sheltered from the airflow. It turned out to be directly behind the high back of the King's saddle and she curled contentedly there on Agranth's firm scales. At one point, apparently of its own accord, the King's right hand slipped down beside the saddle and gently patted the little cloud-hopper warmly on the head. Binnie's heart swelled so much with pride and love for him that she thought it might burst out of her chest with joy. Only the Queen noticed the gesture and she smiled across at Binnie from Cearanth. If Binnie had been furless she would have blushed a bright crimson.

When they finally approached Unicorn Glade the King shouted the order to land at the far end, away from the Unicorns, Naiouli's castle and all the other watching and waiting woodland folk. Puzzled but obedient they all flew in over the elegant building, past Crystal and her herd and touched down lightly, or as lightly as Bizarh could, at the far end of the glade.

"No one is to speak of Goth's treachery," the King said sternly as they gathered together around him. "It will be our secret. It would not do for the people of Elysia to know that their royal family and loyal friends," he lifted his arms to indicate those about him, getting smiles from them all, "were almost all killed. There might be panic. Why, my ministers and advisors might even try to stop my flying." He added in a mock, shocked tone. No one laughed.

"But I am adamant on this," his stern tone returned. "I will of course explain all to Naiouli but no one else need ever know how close we and all Elysia came to disaster. Is that understood?"

A chorus of firm nods was his reply.

"Good." He smiled broadly at them. "Now, let us go and meet with our watchers. Oaken-Pel, Tourmalane, you will please come with me. We have things to discuss." Glancing sideways at Goth he added flatly. "Watch him."

The castle dragons nodded, already positioned as they were on either side of the Dark One.

The Queen clasped her hands together and sighed, falling in behind her husband as they set off across the grass towards a waiting Naiouli.

"Isn't he just a dreamboat when he's being masterful?" she said rapturously to Cearanth, who could only nod dumbly in return.

It was some time later when the royal Elves and their companions re-emerged from Naiouli's castle and walked back across to the waiting dragons and forest dwellers. The only noticeable difference was that Tourmalane once more had his travelling bag with him.

Goth watched their approach in a sullen silence, but some of his smug superiority had returned. He knew they had been deliberating on what to do with him. He also knew that if he had been condemned to death his jurors would have returned almost immediately. But they had not. Whatever they had finally come up with was not fatal and that might give him a second chance, sooner or later, to exact his revenge. Hah! He'd always known the King was soft. Too soft to rule.

The royal Elf in question stopped before his gathered subjects and smiled. This disturbed them slightly but they waited in silence for him to speak.

"My friends," he said warmly. "I know you all want to know what is to be done with Goth." There were many nods and a sneer from the black wizard. The King ignored it. "I cannot have him put to death. It would make me, all of us, a bit more like him. So I have decided to have him returned to his island on the great lake."

"What?" gasped Decorum, for once forgetting who he was talking to.

"But..." Bizarh was confused. The smaller forest dwellers shook their heads in disbelief. Surely the King must realise by now just how dangerous Goth was? Only the royal dragons held their peace. They knew the King better. His Majesty held up a hand and continued as if he had not been interrupted.

"It has already been arranged and, to avoid the chance of any further unpleasantness *en route*, I have asked Naiouli to help with an apparating charm, with which she has kindly obliged."

The mystic stepped forward and bowed gracefully, her palms pressed together in front of her chest.

"Blairoggin, Decorum." The pair snapped to attention at their King's call. "Escort Goth and Tourmalane if you please."

Before they could reply Tourmalane stepped up and stood alongside Goth and the castle dragons took station either side of the pair.

"Watch him," said the King again and dragons turned their full attention to the Dark One.

Naiouli moved smoothly forward until she stood before the group and closed her eyes. Inside everyone's head came faint whispers of some soft incantation that no one understood, then she opened her hands. A glittering, golden thread appeared between them, its ends apparently growing directly out of the soft skin of her palms. It looped outwards, up and over until it completely encircled the two dragons and wizards.

Crack!

With a sound like a whip those within the loop simply disappeared. Naiouli remained holding the empty loop out before her, concentration tight across her usually calm, beautiful features.

The King watched with satisfaction then turned to face the others, his attention focusing on the little forest dwellers. Kizzy, Alcor, Zoozie and Sirus looked eagerly up at their monarch.

"You will all be returned to your friends and family by Blairoggin and Decorum when they return. Is this satisfactory?"

"Oh yes, your Highness." They chorused, smiling shyly at him. He smiled back.

"Your King and your country thank you from the bottom of their hearts for the great service you have done them." He bowed deeply to them all. They couldn't help it, they bowed back. Then he turned to Mira and brave Binnie, who sat at Bizarh's feet.

"I am so sorry for your injuries, little one. And your wings cannot be magicked back. I did ask."

"Thank you, your Majesty." Binnie straightened her sore back and offered up a courageous smile. "It was a small price to pay."

Everyone smiled then and the King knelt down to Binnie's level.

"If you wish you can go back to the forest with your friends too." He knew though that without the ability to fly she would never be able to keep up with all the others or live as she had lived before. "Or you can come and stay in the castle at Talla-Weyre with me. I would be honoured."

Binnie was dumbstruck by the wonderful offer. She stared in amazement at the King.

"Hrumph..." Bizarh cleared his throat noisily. The King and the little cloud-hopper looked up. "Er... if, if it's all right with you Sire, I thought Binnie might like to stay with me."

"For always?" asked Binnie softly, eyes bright with hope and friendship.

Bizarh nodded.

"And Mira too?"

"If she wants. I'd like that."

There was a shy nod from the moonglider and Bizarh smiled warmly down at her. He knew he would never find another friend so brave, smart and true.

"Then it's settled," said the King loudly. He straightened and found himself smiling, along with everybody else.

"But my love." The Queen stepped up beside her husband and looked up at Bizarh. "What are we to do with this handsome forest dragon?" Was there a twinkle in her Majesty's eye?

"Hmmm." The King cupped his chin in one hand. "You are right. We can't have a magnificent and powerful dragon of stature doing nothing and without a master. At least not while I rule Elysia."

A look of panic spread onto Bizarh's face.

"He needs to be taken in hand. And given a task, don't you think?"

His wife, and Oaken-Pel nodded in agreement. If dragons could have sweated, Bizarh would have been sweating now. The King punched a hole in the air before him with a finger, as if suddenly struck by an idea.

"I have the very thing. He can work for me. Yes?" He shot the question at Bizarh.

"Er... er... of, of course. It... it..."

"Good! Now, I shall make a Royal proclamation." He drew himself up to full height. "As my newest dragon, I command you, Bizarh, to patrol these great forests of Elysia. Guard them against my enemies. Be on the lookout for villains, wrong doers and any other sorts of unpleasantness. Take care of my forests for me. Do you think you can do that?"

A tremendous, fanged grin came over Bizarh's face. He too drew himself up to full height, towering over the King.

"With honour and great pleasure, your Majesty."

Everyone laughed and clapped, except Naiouli, who remained motionless, locked in concentration and still holding the magical golden loop out before her.

When the laughter had died down it fell to Agranth to ask the question they all wanted to know the answer to. After all, wasn't the King, Queen, everyone and all Elysia still in danger while Goth lived?

"Your Highness." The greatest dragon in Elysia paused, and looked at his wing as if to emphasise the point he was about to make. "About Goth..."

Everyone's eye was also drawn to the membrane of the wing he now extended, or rather to the neat, round hole burnt through it. The Queen had earlier said to him that she thought the healers back at Talla-Weyre might be able to repair the damage, but Agranth had declined the kind offer. To him his disfigurement was a mark of his devotion to the King. A mark of his personal sacrifice in the protection of his master. But more than that, it was a reminder of the humility and respect he had learned in the last few days and the gained knowledge that how even the smallest, if willing, could make a difference. In a way he now felt more whole with his hole.

"Ah, Goth." The King gave a rueful grin. "Do not worry about him, my friends. I..."

Crack!

Blairoggin, Decorum and Tourmalane, still clutching his now lighter looking bag, re-appeared within the loop of gold thread and Naiouli sighed with relief. She dropped her hands and the thread vaporised around them.

"Is it done?" asked the King.

"Indeed, your Majesty," said Tourmalane, smiling. "Apparating back and forth is rather fun."

But hard work. Naiouli mopped her glistening brow with a delicate charmworm silk hankie which quickly vanished back into the folds of her gossamer gown.

"Are you sure?" the Queen asked the wizard, concern clear in her voice.

Tourmalane nodded emphatically, patting the side of his bag and getting a discreet nod of satisfaction from Oaken-Pel.

"Is what done?" It was of course Bizarh, whose curiosity overrode his deference to the King.

"May I explain?" Tourmalane asked his Majesty and the King smiled his permission.

"Well, it was decided as you know to return Goth to his island. But to ensure that he carried out no more, er, mischief, a little precaution was taken."

"Precaution?" several voices asked together.

"With the help of Naiouli and Oaken-Pel, and a little bit of carbonium, I have put a blanket dampening spell over the area." There were looks of confusion from the dragons and forest dwellers. Tourmalane sighed. He would have to put it simply for the forest people.

"Imagine a great glass dome over Goth's island and the waters around it," he explained. "A magically created glass dome. One that prevents any magic from working. None can go in, none can come out and none can be performed within it. Inside the dome no spells can travel through the air or in, over or through the surrounding water. To all intents and purposes it has totally robbed Goth of his powers. He is no longer a wizard. He simply cannot perform magic and, as the dome is marked against his specific aura, he cannot physically pass through its skin either."

"So he's trapped there on his own horrible island," said Binnie in realisation. "Magic-less."

"Just a plain, boring old bald headed Elf," said Decorum, a smile spreading across his usually stern features.

"Not bad. Not bad at all," said Agranth approvingly, rather louder than he had intended. Cearanth smiled.

The Queen gave the she dragon a reproachful look, dismayed that her own dragon should take pleasure in someone else's discomfort. Even if that someone fully deserved it.

"Well I rather like it too," said the King, winking up at his blood dragon.

"Is it possible he will eventually be able to somehow break through this dampening spell?" asked Blairoggin suddenly, security conscious as only the Keeper of the Keys could be. "He is after all rather clever."

I don't think so. The spell was made by Oaken-Pel, Tourmalane and myself. There was a pause before she explained further. *A tri-spell. And you all know just how difficult they are to correct.*

There were nods of understanding and many looked at the Sword of Elysia, hanging innocently at the King's side, the pommel orb glowing dully in the sunshine.

"Yes." Tourmalane set down his bag and opened his palms. "Goth now has to work for his daily needs, just like any other normal Elf. All he has now is his castle to live in."

"Oh," said Bizarh quietly.

"What?" asked the King, surprised that anyone, especially the green dragon, should show any sympathy or concern over the fate of his former jailer and attacker.

"Did I forget to mention that when we escaped from Goth's castle I... er... accidentally sort of knocked it down." Bizarh looked sheepishly at those around him.

There was a moment's stunned silence.

"Couldn't have happened to a nicer Elf," said Decorum quietly, then everyone in Unicorn Glade burst into laughter.

And far away, on a mist shrouded island in the middle of a grey lake Goth shook his clenched fist up at the imprisoning air around him. Then his angry face cracked into one of despair. He clapped his hands to the sides of his bald head and sank to his knees.

A wailing cry could be heard across the flat, still waters.

"NOooo......."

COMING UP ROSES